A THIEF IN THEIR MIDST . . .

"I have a very disturbing announcement to make," began Max. "Someone has just taken a large sum of money out of my office."

The crowd began to murmur. Max held up his hand for silence. "It was my fault for being so careless as to leave it there, but I've always encouraged an open atmosphere at this stable and I didn't think it would be a problem. Now the money is gone, and if anyone knows anything about the disappearance, please come and talk to me. If you know where the money is, you can just leave it in my office when I'm not there—no questions asked."

The riders from visiting Pony Clubs shuffled uneasily, and several people darted glances at each other. Then Veronica diAngelo stepped forward.

"I know something. I know who took the money," she announced. "Phil Marsten is the thief. I saw him sneaking out of your office ten minutes ago!"

THE SADDLE CLUB

HORSE THIEF

BONNIE BRYANT

A SKYLARK BOOK
NEW YORK · TORONTO · LONDON · SYDNEY · AUCKLAND

RL 5, 009–012

HORSE THIEF

A Bantam Skylark Book / October 1998

ISBN 0-553-48633-0

Published simultaneously in the United States and Canada.

PRINTED IN THE UNITED STATES OF AMERICA

OPM   0 9 8 7 6 5 4 3 2

*I would like to express my special thanks
to Minna Jung for her help
in the writing of this book.*

STEVIE LAKE SHIFTED uncomfortably. The floor in Max's office seemed to be getting harder, and she was squeezed next to one of her best friends, Carole Hanson. She dug her elbow into Carole's side and whispered, "Move over. My foot is falling asleep."

Without budging an inch, Carole absently whispered back, "Shhh. I can't hear what Doc Tock is saying."

Stevie grinned. Normally Carole couldn't think about anything but horses. Her head swam with bits of advice about riding, grooming, and anything else to do with horse care. Stevie's other best friend, Lisa Atwood, was sitting on the other side of Carole and looked just as absorbed as Carole did. The three girls were not only best friends, but they also shared a love of horses, which had

1

led them to form The Saddle Club. The only requirements for joining were that members had to be crazy about horses and had to be willing to help one another out.

But at today's unmounted meeting of Horse Wise, the Pony Club all three girls belonged to, the topic for discussion had nothing to do with horses. Usually Max Regnery, the leader of Horse Wise and the owner of Pine Hollow Stables, where Horse Wise members rode, used these unmounted meetings to discuss some aspect of stable management. For this meeting, however, Max had invited Doc Tock—everybody's nickname for Dr. Takamura—to update Horse Wise about the latest efforts of the County Animal Rescue League, or CARL. Almost everyone in Horse Wise knew about CARL's work saving abused or injured animals and finding them new homes or, in the case of wild animals, returning them safely to the wild. Doc Tock was a veterinarian who donated medical care to animals rescued by CARL, and her daughter, Corey, was a member of Horse Wise.

Carole, Lisa, and Stevie had participated in Horse Wise riding exhibitions to raise money for CARL's work. They loved hearing about the animals rescued by CARL, even when it meant sitting on the hard floor in Max's office for half an hour, and *even* if it meant that the topic for discussion wasn't horses.

Stevie decided to ignore the pins and needles in her

foot and concentrate on what Doc Tock was saying. ". . . and the building was scheduled to be demolished, so volunteers from CARL went in as soon as we could get permission and managed to capture her."

Stevie nudged Phil Marsten, her boyfriend, who was her guest for the meeting. " 'Her'?" she whispered.

"Pregnant fox . . . abandoned building . . . needed rescuing," Phil whispered back.

A pregnant fox! Stevie had seen a few foxes around Willow Creek, the town where they lived, and she knew that they were common in the Virginia countryside. She remembered once seeing a fox's bushy tail disappear into a thicket while she and Lisa and Carole were on a trail ride. She had even played one once, when she had been chosen to be the fox in a mock foxhunt. Although she had received a lot of ribbing about playing a fox, she was glad they hadn't chased a *real* one.

"I bet fox babies are cute," Stevie whispered to Phil. Then she caught Max's stern glance and immediately looked contrite. Max hated it when riders talked during meetings and lessons.

"The most important thing about wild animal rescues," continued Doc Tock, "is that we don't treat the animals like pets. We don't try to build their trust in us, because we want them to return to their natural environment, so they can't become too familiar with humans. Sometimes an animal's fear of humans is what saves its life. So we rescued the fox, fed her well to build up her strength and prepare her for giving birth, then released her in the state park—far away from any more abandoned buildings. Unfortunately, wild animals do sometimes find their way into human areas, which is a sign that civilization is crowding out their natural habitats. A good example of this is raccoons, which can sometimes be found rummaging through people's garbage cans. Raccoons will eat anything, and they can make quite a mess."

Doc Tock concluded, "Now we're hoping that the fox safely gave birth to her kits in the park. She's probably wishing she had a baby-sitter right about now!"

"What's her hourly rate?" Stevie asked.

Everyone laughed. Then Max stepped forward, holding a glass jar. "I'm leaving this jar in the locker room," he announced. "If you have any spare change rattling around in your pockets, you may want to drop it in the jar. When the jar is full, we'll give it to CARL to help support their work."

Spare change was something Stevie rarely had. Although her parents were fairly well off, they were also pretty firm about Stevie's allowance. Stevie had three brothers, and four children meant that the Lake household had a lot of expenses. Stevie was expected to help around the house to earn her allowance—and she had to help with the cost of keeping her horse at Pine Hollow. Unless it was for a really special occasion, her parents

4

didn't give her extra spending money. They were all too familiar with their daughter's crazy spending habits—and crazy ideas. Money just didn't seem to stay in Stevie's pockets for long, but she hoped she could manage to save some for the CARL jar.

The meeting was over, and everyone started filing out. Stevie stood up and stretched. She tapped the rag rug with her foot. "I think Max needs a nice thick plush carpet in his office," she complained. "This little rug didn't help my backside one bit!"

Phil laughed. "Yeah, that would be practical," he teased. "With riders tramping through here all day, tracking in dirt from the ring."

Carole and Lisa laughed, too. They couldn't imagine Max's no-nonsense, no-frills office with a fancy rug, either. The only decorations in the office were a few photographs of champion horses and riders that Max had ridden or helped train and a photograph on his desk of his wife, Deborah, and their daughter, Maxi.

Stevie put on a fake mad expression and punched Phil lightly in the arm. "Just remember, Phil, that you're my guest here today," she told him. "That means you have to be extra nice to me."

"No, I'm the guest, remember?" Phil answered. "*You've* got to be nice to *me*."

"Why don't you two just be nice to each other?" Carole broke in impatiently. She and Lisa had spent a lot of time with Stevie and Phil and knew that they were prone to playful, competitive bickering. Unfortunately, once they got started, they kept on going. Carole tugged on Stevie's arm and said, "C'mon, you two. We have a lot to do this afternoon."

The group planned to spend the afternoon practicing for a Pony Club dressage rally that was going to be held at Pine Hollow the following Saturday. The rally was to be staged just like a real dressage competition, with tests on different types of dressage steps. Max had invited a well-known rider from the United States Dressage Federation to come and judge the event.

Phil's Pony Club, Cross County, was also going to participate in the rally. Phil had had his horse, Teddy, brought over to Pine Hollow that day so that he could practice with Stevie.

Everyone in Horse Wise was excited about the rally, but Stevie was especially looking forward to the event. Dressage, which involved very technical but balletic riding without jumping, was one of her favorite events. It always amazed people who knew Stevie and her flamboyant tendencies to see how she excelled at this precise and demanding form of horsemanship. She practiced dressage movements with her part-Arabian horse, Belle, whenever she could, and she really wanted to win a ribbon in the competition.

* * *

A FEW MINUTES later, Stevie finished tacking up and headed to the indoor ring. On the way out she passed by Prancer's stall, where she saw Lisa standing by the mare, looking puzzled.

Unlike Carole and Stevie, Lisa didn't own a horse, but she almost always rode the same Pine Hollow horse, Prancer, an ex-racehorse and a Thoroughbred. Although the mare was sometimes flighty and high-strung, Lisa loved her long, graceful lines and smooth gaits. Right now, however, she had a discouraged expression on her face and was shaking her head.

Stevie halted Belle. "What's up?" she asked.

"Something's wrong with Prancer," Lisa replied, patting the horse reassuringly. "I can't put my finger on it, but she's acting a little strange."

"Strange how?" asked Carole, who had come up behind Stevie and was leading Starlight, her bay gelding. "Is her appetite okay? Does her coat look healthy? Has she been lying down and getting up? Is she coughing?"

Despite her worry, Lisa couldn't help smiling. Carole was so horse-crazy that she was prone to deliver lengthy lectures about riding and horse management. Her barrage of questions, Lisa knew, came from her extensive knowledge about illnesses like colic, which was the general term for a variety of intestinal problems in horses. Because horses lacked the ability to regurgitate their food, intestinal problems could be serious; Carole's questions covered a checklist of colic's deadly symptoms.

Prancer, however, didn't have any of the symptoms of colic. She wasn't looking toward her flank or getting up and lying down. She looked exactly the same as always. Lisa shook her head again. "She doesn't look sick," she said. "She just hasn't been herself for the last few days. When she sees me, she gives me strange looks, and she seems a little less energetic than usual. But otherwise, she looks great."

Carole handed Starlight's reins to Stevie and came into the stall with Lisa. She had spent a lot of time helping out Judy Barker, the local equine veterinarian, and had witnessed and assisted in many examinations of horses. She checked over Prancer carefully. "I can't see anything wrong with her," Carole said. "But you know her best, Lisa. Maybe you should talk to Max."

Lisa nodded. "I'll ask Max to call Judy. I'm certainly not going to take any chances. Maybe it's just the weather—I know it's getting *me* down. One more day of rain and I personally will be on the lookout for an ark."

Willow Creek had had a lot of rain recently. The girls had wanted to practice outdoors after the meeting, and they thought a trail ride after the practice might do the horses some good. Horses, like people, could get cabin fever from being cooped up too long. But the outdoor ring and the trails were slick with mud, so the girls would be practicing in the indoor ring.

Lisa finished tightening Prancer's girth and led her out of the stall. She felt slightly better now that she had decided to ask Max to call Judy.

The three girls met Phil and Teddy in the indoor ring and began practicing lateral work. Lateral work involved turns and steps where the horse moved forward and sideways. In one lateral exercise, the leg yield, the horse moved forward and sideways while bent very slightly away from the direction of movement. The group then took turns practicing gait changes, which was also an important element of dressage tests.

During their practice sessions, the girls often helped each other out with advice about riding. Sometimes a rider could get so wrapped up in what he or she was doing that it could become difficult to correct mistakes or bad habits. And sometimes it helped a rider to know that he or she was doing something right. For this reason, The Saddle Club often took turns executing different steps and formations so that the others could praise or critique the person doing the riding.

As the practice session went on, Carole and Lisa couldn't help noticing that Stevie and Phil seemed to be complimenting one another above and beyond the call of duty. In fact, they were being extremely helpful and supportive of one another, commenting on every little thing that the other did well.

"Great flying change, Phil!" Stevie called out. For flying change, a horse changed leads in midcanter. "I couldn't even tell when you gave Teddy the cue!"

Phil grinned happily, patting Teddy on the neck. In dressage, a rider tried to make the aids—the commands to his horse—nearly invisible. Carole and Lisa expected Phil to boast about the training he had been giving Teddy, but instead he kept on beaming at Stevie. "Belle looks terrific," he said. "Those suppling exercises must really be working!"

Dressage often involved bends of a horse's body or quick footwork, and riders could improve their horses' flexibility through suppling exercises. Stevie spent a lot of time on these exercises, which included transitions between gaits and moving Belle sideways with leg commands. Sometimes the exercises involved bending a horse's body in ways that the horse was unaccustomed to, so the rider had to be extra patient and gentle when teaching a horse how to do them. Suppling exercises not only helped a horse train for dressage, they also helped improve the horse's agility for all forms of riding.

Carole and Lisa waited off to the side while Stevie and Phil practiced dressage movements involving cantering. After Phil complimented Stevie on her posture, Carole turned to Lisa, her eyebrows raised. "Do you hear what I

10

hear? I feel like I'm watching a class on how to have a successful relationship."

"I know," Lisa said, nodding. "They're acting like the model couple." She gagged jokingly. "Is this the same couple we know and love?"

Both Carole and Lisa knew that Stevie, in addition to being imaginative and fun, could be supercompetitive, a quality she shared with her boyfriend. Her competitive nature helped make her a good rider, but it also made her a pain to be around sometimes, especially when she and Phil were competing against one another. Phil lived in a nearby town, so he and Stevie didn't get to see each other as often as they would've liked. Unfortunately, when they did get together, they often found themselves pitted against one another. The two of them sometimes made bets with each other about who would win what rally, whose horse was better, who was a better rider, or who had discovered the latest training technique. At times the competition between Stevie and Phil resulted in not-so-smart choices—like the time Stevie had almost overtrained Belle to learn a dressage movement that Phil and Teddy had already mastered.

For the past several months, however, the couple had been remarkably squabble-free. They still argued over minor things, but their competition with each other seemed to have died down. Crossing her fingers, Carole commented, "Let's just hope this little phase lasts. Forever."

"Amen," said Lisa. "Even this gooey sweetness is better than what they used to be like."

"Are you guys talking about us?" demanded Stevie, riding up.

"Yes," Carole replied promptly. "We're talking about how you guys are so much more fun now that you've stopped trying to kill each other in competition."

Lisa rolled her eyes and nodded.

Phil had joined them and overheard Carole's comment. "Oh, c'mon, we gave that up ages ago," he protested.

"We're much more mature now," added Stevie. Her serious expression made Carole and Lisa want to giggle, but they managed to keep straight faces. They knew how difficult it was for Stevie and Phil to suppress their natural competitive spirits when they were with each other. Aside from their competitiveness, however, Stevie and Phil made a perfect couple. They both had a great sense of adventure and were always coming up with fun things to do.

"In fact, next week we're even celebrating six months of our not competing," Stevie announced proudly. She smiled at Phil, who blushed a little and smiled back.

Carole and Lisa were properly impressed. "Wow. Six months," commented Lisa. "What are you going to do, go out for a fancy dinner?"

"Are you kidding?" groaned Stevie. "I can barely afford a TD's sundae, let alone a fancy dinner. I'm totally broke. I can't even buy the things I need for riding."

"Like what?" Carole asked. Stevie never seemed to care much for fancy riding equipment. She usually wore old jeans and T-shirts with cowboy boots that had seen better days, and she was the first person to admit that she preferred comfort over glamor.

"Well, I guess I don't *need* anything exactly," admitted Stevie. "But my old bridle looks really beat up, and I would love to get a new snaffle bridle. I don't want a double snaffle, the kind with four reins. The guy at the tack store said I wouldn't need a double bridle unless I was in international competition—and I'm certainly not there yet. But even simple snaffle bridles are really expensive—over a hundred dollars! There's no way I can buy one before next Saturday."

Carole and Lisa nodded understandingly. Now everything was much clearer. Even though Stevie was less than serious about a lot of things, she became very focused when it came to dressage tack and appearance. She always dressed impeccably for dressage events, and she trained with special equipment that Carole and Lisa didn't have—like a dressage riding whip. Dressage whips were longer, easier to handle, and more elegant-looking than regular riding crops. Snaffle bridles had reins attached directly to the ring of the bit. This established a direct line of communication between the rider and the horse.

"That's tough," Phil told Stevie. "But I know what you mean. I've been trying to earn extra money lately from odd jobs, and it takes forever to save up any decent amount. Mowing lawns, weeding—no job is too small for Phil Marsten. Although," he added ruefully, "it seems like the *pay* is always too small."

"Why do you need so much extra money?" Lisa asked curiously.

"Oh, I decided to switch feed suppliers," Phil answered. "I'm still giving Teddy the usual stuff, but I decided to try this feed supplier who said he had a better quality of hay. I want to give Teddy the best kind of food there is, since he eats like . . . like a horse."

The three girls burst into laughter. They knew that Phil took excellent care of Teddy, fussing over him like a parent with a new baby. As a result, the horse was clearly healthy, content, and well muscled.

"Well, I think that right about now, I could eat like a horse, too," announced Carole. "We've been practicing for two hours. Let's call it a day and go get a snack."

"TD's!" said Stevie. It was a natural suggestion. TD's (short for Tastee Delight) was a nearby ice cream parlor where the trio often held impromptu Saddle Club meetings.

After making sure the horses were cooled down, the group headed back to the stable. Phil and the girls watered and groomed the horses and automatically carried their tack to the tack room for cleaning. Max and his mother, Mrs. Reg, had given too many lectures about taking care of their riding equipment for the group to leave dirty tack lying around.

In the tack room, they ran into Denise McCaskill. Denise taught part-time at Pine Hollow and was also an A-rated Pony Club member. She was majoring in equine studies at a Virginia college and was dating Red O'Malley, Pine Hollow's head stable hand. Denise was looking over the equipment in the tack room and writing things down in a notebook. She looked distracted and was mumbling to herself.

Lisa tapped her on the shoulder. "Hi, Denise."

Denise jumped a little, then smiled when she saw the girls and Phil. "Oh, hi," she said tiredly. She brushed her hair out of her eyes, yawned, then accidentally dropped her notebook.

Carole picked it up and handed it back to her. "Are you okay?" she asked. It was completely unlike calm, efficient Denise to look so frazzled.

"I guess I am a little out of it," sighed Denise. "Max hired me to do some extra work to plan for the rally next week, and I was just checking over the equipment to make sure everything looks okay."

15

"You look really tired," Stevie said bluntly.

"Thanks a lot," said Denise, looking both amused and insulted.

"I didn't mean you look terrible," Stevie amended sheepishly. "You just look like you haven't gotten enough sleep lately."

"How do you find the time to work on the rally?" asked Carole. The Saddle Club had helped Max prepare for exhibitions and rallies before, and they knew how time-consuming such preparation could be. "Aren't you busy with your college courses?"

Denise sighed again. "Busy doesn't even begin to describe it," she said wearily. "I've got two papers due next week and a midterm exam. But I asked Max if he would hire me for this because, frankly, I need the extra money. I just got a letter informing me that the college is raising tuition—again. This is the third or fourth time they've done that, and I just didn't budget for the steep increases. I don't know how I'm going to make ends meet."

Impulsively, Lisa gave Denise a quick hug. "Listen, *we'll* help you prepare for the rally," she promised. "That way you'll have more time to study." Carole, Stevie, and Phil nodded in agreement. One of the Saddle Club rules was that members had to help each other out, and the girls often found themselves extending that help to other people, too. Sometimes the results were mixed, but their intentions were always good.

Denise smiled gratefully. "Thanks," she replied. "I know I can count on you guys. If you could ask Mrs. Reg what we're doing about refreshments for the rally, I'd be really grateful. I also need someone to talk to Max or Red about where we're going to put the guest riders and horses."

Just then, Veronica diAngelo sauntered into the tack room. "Denise, where's Red? My new dressage bridle seems to have a loose rein. I need him to mend it for me, right away. Goodness," she added with a light laugh, "money doesn't really buy anything these days, does it? I may have to buy a new one already!"

Carole, Lisa, and Stevie glared at the other girl. None of them could stand Veronica, whose incredibly wealthy parents seemed to give her anything she wanted. She was undoubtedly the most spoiled member of Horse Wise, and she was the worst behaved. Besides throwing tantrums until she got her own way or flaunting her latest piece of riding equipment, Veronica never bothered to look after her horse or clean her own tack. She simply commanded Red to do it for her. The Saddle Club avoided her whenever they could, but at a close-knit stable like Pine Hollow, that was sometimes difficult.

Now Veronica was dragging a brand-new dressage bridle—exactly the kind that Stevie wanted. It didn't appear to have the slightest thing wrong with it except that it was covered in dust. The fact that Veronica could just

17

buy another bridle whenever she wanted made Stevie grit her teeth. She couldn't help—just for a second—coveting Veronica's unlimited spending allowance. *But if I had her money*, Stevie comforted herself, *I'd probably turn out to be a spoiled brat like her.*

Veronica began talking about the new dressage bridle and saddle that she was planning to buy in time for Saturday's rally. Everyone except Veronica noticed the grim expression on Denise's face.

Stevie started to say something, but Phil beat her to it. "Oh Veronica, dahling," he drawled. "I saw this diamond-studded saddle—with stirrups of pure gold, no less—that would be simply perfect for you. It's an absolute *must-have* for fancy-pants riders. I'm sure you won't be able to *live* with yourself until you get it."

Carole, Lisa, and Stevie started giggling at Phil's little recital. Even Denise smiled a little.

Veronica, though, was furious. She started to say something but then caught a glimpse of Denise's smile, which made her turn bright red in embarrassment. Veronica admired Denise because of her Pony Club credentials—in Veronica's mind, Denise's A rating was all that mattered. The fact that Denise had witnessed her humiliation made Veronica even madder. She glowered at Phil and said threateningly, "Just you wait, Phil Marsten. I'll make you eat your words next week at the rally! No one will ever talk to you again when I'm through with you!" With that, she stormed out of the tack room.

Lisa looked worried. "What do you suppose Veronica is going to do?" she asked.

"A great big nothing," said Stevie in a disgusted tone. "She thinks she's going to beat Phil in the competition, but that's impossible. Phil's a much better rider than Veronica."

This wasn't entirely true. Although Phil was a very good rider, Veronica was, too, and her father's money had helped her acquire a very fine horse, Danny, who always did the right thing with or without Veronica's help.

Nevertheless, Carole and Lisa loyally agreed with Stevie. All four said good-bye to Denise and headed off to talk to Mrs. Reg, who helped run the stable. They were all looking forward to their sweet snack at TD's—anything to take away the bad taste of Veronica.

"I DON'T KNOW what we should do for our anniversary celebration," Stevie said into the phone. "I keep hoping that maybe I'll hit the lottery, and then I can treat us to a really terrific dinner and a fancy show with a limo thrown in for good measure."

On the other end, Phil chuckled. "You never *play* the lottery," he said. "I'm pretty sure you have to play to win. It's all a big waste of money, anyway. Most people spend a fortune on tickets without ever seeing a dime."

"I guess," Stevie said sadly. She certainly didn't want to waste any more money. But she also wanted a good get-rich-quick scheme, preferably one that would make her rich in a day or two. It was Wednesday, and the dressage rally was only three days away. *Even if I hadn't* spent half my allowance on TD's and that cool electronic-buzzer keychain that I didn't really need, I still wouldn't have been able to buy that new snaffle bridle, she reminded herself. But she didn't feel any better.

"Stevie, have you gone off to Mars?" Phil asked with a slight hint of impatience.

"I'm sorry," Stevie said, returning to earth. "I just went off to tack heaven for a few seconds. You know—the place in the sky where you get all your riding equipment, brand-new and for free."

"Very funny," said Phil. He sounded a little miffed. "Are you still thinking about that bridle?"

"Yes, but it's pointless," sighed Stevie. "I'm not going to be able to get it before Saturday, or even in the next century, if I keep spending money the way I do. What were you saying?"

"I was trying to discuss our anniversary plans," Phil said pointedly. "I wanted to know how you felt about dinner after the dressage rally."

"Are you out of your skull?" Stevie demanded. "We were just talking about how broke we both are!"

"No, no," said Phil, his voice reassuring. "I've been thinking about it, Stevie, and I know a way to do it without spending a lot of money. I'll pack a picnic dinner for us—my mother promised to give me her secret chicken salad recipe. We can eat on the lawn at Pine Hollow after the rally. I'll bring a blanket and candles and everything. I've already cleared it with Max. What do you think?"

Stevie thought it was a great idea. Even though she and Phil had been going out for a long time, she sometimes felt as if their relationship was entirely centered on horses and riding. But every once in a while, Phil surprised her with something incredibly romantic like this picnic idea. "I'm very glad to know you, Phil Marsten," she said solemnly. "And to show you how glad I am, I'll help with the picnic dinner. Just tell me what to bring."

"Uh, no thanks, Stevie," Phil answered quickly. "Not to knock your cooking or anything, but I really think we want something . . . er . . . more ordinary than your usual meals."

"What's wrong with my usual meals?" Stevie demanded indignantly, though she had an idea of what was on his mind. She liked to think of her kitchen failures as *interesting,* though that wasn't the word her friends chose to describe her dishes.

"I've seen those awful sundaes you eat at TD's," Phil replied. "And something lurks in my memory about green hamburgers. I think we'll do better if you just sit back and let me take care of you this time. One can't live on romance alone—and my stomach will certainly confirm that fact."

Stevie giggled. "I'm sure you'll be getting more than a little help from your mother, but I appreciate the thought," she said. "I'll talk to you tomorrow. And Phil," she added softly, "you're the greatest."

After they hung up, Stevie wandered over to her closet. If she had been excited about the dressage rally before, now she could hardly wait for Saturday. First she would compete in the rally itself, and then she would have a romantic picnic dinner with Phil. She looked over her riding clothes and picked out her best jacket, her best pair of breeches, and her white stock tie. No cowboy boots for Saturday, no jeans with patches on them. She and her horse had to look their best, and she planned to put in some extra time grooming Belle that week.

Thinking about the dressage bridle, Stevie became glum again. The chance of her getting one before the rally was looking pretty slim. But she had ridden in plenty of dressage exhibitions and rallies with her old bridle, and she figured that she would just do it again.

She stuck her head out her bedroom door. "Mom!" she yelled. "Can you please help me iron my tie for Saturday?" With or without a new bridle, Stevie planned to be prepared.

THE NEXT DAY, Carole, Lisa, and Stevie all gathered after school for another dressage practice.

After practicing for two hours, The Saddle Club walked their horses to cool them down. As usual, they talked as they walked. The horses seemed to listen, too,

23

twitching their ears back at different parts of the conversation. "How's Prancer doing? Is she still acting funny?" Carole asked Lisa.

Lisa frowned. "Judy came and took a look at her on Monday," she said. "She couldn't find anything wrong with her, so she told me to keep a close eye on her and call if anything specific happens."

Carole nodded. "Like not finishing her food or nipping at her flanks?" she guessed.

"Exactly," Lisa said glumly.

"Why are you frowning, then?" Stevie asked. "Prancer's fine."

Shaking her head, Lisa said, "No, she's not. I know that medically she's okay, and I'm relieved. But she's not acting like her usual self. She's just been in a weird mood lately."

Carole and Stevie didn't doubt Lisa for a second. She might be the least experienced rider out of the three of them, but she was also the most sensible and logical and wasn't given to paranoid hunches. Plus, she rode Prancer more than any other rider at Pine Hollow. If anyone could sense a change in the mare, Lisa could.

After their horses were cooled and groomed, the girls gathered in the tack room. Cleaning tack seemed a never-ending task, since it had to be done after each use. While they rubbed their saddles with saddle soap, they talked about what they were going to wear for the dressage rally and speculated on the competition. Then Stevie talked about Phil's idea for their anniversary celebration.

"You are one lucky girlfriend," Carole said admiringly. Even though she was usually more interested in horses than boys, she was impressed by Phil's romantic idea.

"I know," Stevie said. "I can hardly wait for Saturday. Even if I won't have a new dressage bridle, I'm sure the whole day will be a blast."

At that moment, the three girls overheard Max in his office, talking in a loud, annoyed voice to his mother. "I can't take it anymore," he was saying. "At least a third of the hay delivered this afternoon was rotten. The supplier obviously left it out in the rain. It was musty and smelled awful, completely unfit for horses."

Mrs. Reg said something in a soothing tone that the girls couldn't quite catch.

"No, no, no," Max answered impatiently. "I've already given him a few chances, so don't give me any stories about people learning from their mistakes! Feed is just too important to mess around with. I'm going to call him up and demand a refund for the spoiled portion, then switch back to Mike Morgan. He's more expensive, but it's worth it. I'm sorry I ever switched in the first place."

The girls heard Max pick up the phone and dial a

number and then begin to speak in firm, decisive tones. Stevie shook her head. "Brother," she said, in a low voice. "Running a stable is hard work."

"You said it," agreed Carole. She sometimes dreamed of owning a stable someday, but she knew that a lot of thought and planning went into running a place like Pine Hollow. In fact, making decisions about things like feed suppliers and money seemed like the most boring thing about owning a stable. Cleaning tack, by comparison, was almost fun.

"I haven't noticed anything wrong with the feed, have you?" Stevie asked.

"No," Lisa said. "But then Max checks it over before it gets put in the stable. We'd never know anything was wrong because he does such a good job."

The three girls went back to discussing the upcoming rally and Stevie's picnic. They could hardly wait for Saturday.

"WHAT A GORGEOUS day!" exclaimed Stevie. Pine Hollow, which was always beautiful to those who loved it, almost glowed in the sunshine. After what had felt like weeks of rain, Saturday had dawned bright and clear. The mugginess had lifted, and a few white clouds dotted a breathtakingly blue sky. The girls were sure it was an omen and that the rally would be as perfect as the weather.

Stevie, Carole, and Lisa were in the stable, grooming their horses. Although it was still a few hours before the rally, The Saddle Club had agreed to get to Pine Hollow especially early to get the horses into show condition and to help Denise with last-minute preparations for guests and spectators.

"You can't ask for a better day for dressage," said Carole. She was carefully oiling one of Starlight's hooves.

Lisa didn't say anything. She was examining Prancer. The mare looked healthy, but something was still wrong. She kept poking her nose over the door of her stall as if she expected something. Lisa had a hard time getting her to stand still as she groomed her. If she didn't know better, she would almost guess that Prancer looked as if she were *yearning* for something. She was a little fidgety, too, but that wasn't uncommon for Prancer. "What is it, girl?" Lisa asked the horse. "What can I do for you that I haven't already done?" The mare shook her head and snorted.

Stevie started braiding Belle's mane. She brushed it with a wet brush and divided it into twelve even sections. Then she neatly divided each section into three smaller sections, braided the three sections together, then looped the braid under and sewed it tight with yarn. Stevie could be a messy person about many things—her parents had labeled her room a disaster area on several occasions—but not about dressage preparation. Her boots gleamed and her stock tie was perfectly pressed.

"Stevie," called Lisa, "I can't get my sections even!"

"Stevie," called Carole, "can you help me sew this one section? I can't seem to tuck it under!" Dressage preparation was one of the few areas concerning riding where

28

Carole ended up asking Stevie for advice, instead of the other way around.

"Just a second," Stevie answered. She finished sewing the seventh section of Belle's mane and then realized with dismay that she was out of yarn. Although dressage riders sometimes used colored yarn, colors tended to accentuate any unevenness in braiding. Stevie was using black yarn—the same color as Belle's mane. "Help!" she said to Lisa. "I'm out of yarn!"

"No problem," replied Lisa. "I brought extra." She came out of Prancer's stall and tossed a ball over the stall door.

"I have some more, too," Carole called, tossing her ball lightly over her horse's back.

"Thanks," said Stevie, deftly catching both balls of yarn as they came sailing her way. Since Prancer and Starlight were bays, like Belle, Carole and Lisa were also using black yarn. "You guys are lifesavers."

"Well, don't think we don't expect something in return," said Lisa.

"Like braiding lessons," declared Carole.

"At your service," said Stevie. "As soon as I finish up with Belle."

Stevie finished braiding Belle's mane and then neatly braided her forelock and along the length of the dock of her tail. She stepped back and admired her work. "You look gorgeous!" she told Belle. The mare nickered in response.

Then Stevie helped Carole and Lisa finish their braiding. The three horses looked beautiful; they tossed their heads as if they had just dressed up for a special occasion. "Sometimes I think Belle is one vain horse," confided Stevie to her friends, who laughed and agreed.

Since the rally was still a couple of hours away, the girls didn't tack up the horses just yet. Instead, they wandered outside into the brilliant morning sunshine. Riders and horses from other stables were beginning to arrive, and the scene was one of increasing confusion. Stevie recognized the Marstens' van as it pulled into Pine Hollow's driveway, and she and Carole and Lisa walked over to greet Phil.

Phil jumped out of the van and waved hello. He pulled a large picnic hamper out of the backseat and turned to give Stevie a hug. "I can't wait for our picnic dinner tonight," he told her. "When I woke up this morning and saw what a beautiful day it was, I gave a yell that woke my whole house up. My sisters still aren't speaking to me."

Stevie hugged Phil back, but she couldn't help frowning just a little. She was excited about their picnic, too—she loved doing things like that with Phil. And the hamper certainly looked inviting. She wondered what Phil had managed to squeeze in there. But they had a dressage rally to compete in before getting to the picnic, and Stevie, for one, was still determined to win a ribbon.

Nevertheless, she was flattered. "I'm excited, too," she said. "Let's go stow the hamper at Max's."

Just then A.J., another rider from Cross County and a good friend of Phil's, joined them. He had driven over with the Marstens, and his horse was also in the trailer. "Uh, Phil, can I have a second?" he inquired.

Phil still had his arm around Stevie. "Yeah?" he answered distractedly.

"Remember what we brought with us? You know, those four-legged animals that we plan on riding today? Do you think maybe you could give me a hand with unloading?" A.J. asked, grinning.

The girls laughed, and Phil did, too, after blushing a little. "Sorry, A.J.," he said.

"We'll help," offered Carole. "Our horses are groomed and almost ready to go."

As they were unbolting the trailer door, Denise and Red hurried past them toward the stable. "What's the rush, Denise?" called Carole. "Can we help?"

Denise skidded to a stop. She still looked worried and tired, but she smiled at the group. "Those are the sweetest words I know!" she said. "And the answer is yes. I have to go to the stable with Red and take care of something. If you could help unload the trailers of the arriving Pony Clubs, and then show them where to put

31

their horses before the rally begins, I'd really appreciate it."

"No problem," Carole answered promptly.

Denise thanked them and hurried after Red.

As the girls watched them go, the reason for their haste became apparent. Veronica stood in the doorway of the stable, holding the halter of her blue-blooded, light gray horse, Danny. She tapped her toe impatiently when she saw Denise and Red coming toward her.

"There you are," the girls heard her say. "Danny's mane is a mess, and he needs a thorough grooming! Where have you been? Am I expected to do everything myself around here?"

"Honestly!" Lisa said in disgust. "Veronica continues to amaze me! She manages to monopolize Denise *and* Red on a day when they're both incredibly busy. Why does Max let her get away with it?"

"You know Veronica's parents pay a lot of extra money for Danny's care," Carole reminded Lisa. "Plus they're so well known and influential in this town, Max can't afford to make them angry. He needs their referrals to entice new riders. But Veronica could certainly stand a personality transplant."

The five friends started to unload Phil's and A.J.'s horses but paused when they saw Veronica strolling toward them. She had obviously left Danny under the care of Denise and Red, so now she could relax and start annoying other people. Her expression turned sour when she looked at Phil.

Phil didn't miss a beat. He turned his nose up again and said helpfully, "Veronica, perhaps you shouldn't compete in the rally today."

Veronica stopped. "Why?" she demanded.

"Because you're obviously too good for us," Phil replied, grinning.

Veronica looked confused. She couldn't tell if Phil was teasing her again or flattering her.

"In fact," Phil continued, "I think you're just *too good* for this entire stable. I mean, you're obviously too good to groom your own horse or take care of your own tack. Perhaps you're just too good to do . . . anything at all."

Veronica didn't say a word. She turned on her heel and flounced off in the opposite direction.

"Phil, maybe you shouldn't tease her so much," said Lisa, worried. "Veronica can be pretty nasty when she's upset."

Phil shrugged. "I think I can handle her," he said.

AFTER HELPING PHIL and A.J. unload their horses, Carole, Lisa, and Stevie began greeting new arrivals, helping them unload their horses and directing the cars and trailers toward the parking area. The Pony Club from Mendenhall Stables was the first to arrive. Because Mendenhall was located over an hour away, Horse Wise rarely competed against them at local riding events. They had met only one or two of their riders before.

Lisa approached a tall, skinny boy with brown floppy hair. He was unloading a bay gelding, which was backing out of the trailer docilely.

Lisa was impressed. "Hi, I'm Lisa," she introduced herself. "Can I give you a hand? I can show you where the guest riders and horses are supposed to go."

The boy glanced at her, then his eyes darted nervously away. "No thanks, I can find it," he muttered.

Lisa was slightly taken aback. "What's your name?" she asked politely.

The boy looked at her again, and Lisa could swear that he seemed dismayed that she hadn't gone away. "Kurt," he muttered. He still hadn't returned her welcoming smile.

Maybe Kurt is shy, Lisa thought. She remembered how strange she had felt the first time she had ridden at a stable other than Pine Hollow. She had taken part in a show at Tapert Crest, a nearby stable. Pine Hollow had become such a familiar place to her that she had felt disoriented at first, even with Carole and Stevie there. But she remembered how some riders from Tapert Crest had welcomed her and that it had really made her day.

She tried again. In her friendliest tone, she said, "I ride with Horse Wise, the club here at Pine Hollow. I'm also helping out with the rally, since we're the hosts. Can I show you and your horse to the indoor ring? Do you need help carrying your tack?"

"No," Kurt said briefly.

Lisa was starting to get discouraged. Kurt, she thought, was certainly living up to his name! She made one last attempt to draw him out. "Your horse is so well behaved," she said admiringly. "I've seen horses that refuse to go in and out of trailers without a lot of fuss, you know? You must spend an awful lot of time riding and training him."

Awkwardly, Kurt attached a lead rein to his horse's halter. "Not really," he said. "Now if you'll excuse me, Simon needs some warming up." He turned his back on Lisa and the message was unmistakable: Leave me alone.

Lisa, irritated at Kurt's astonishing rudeness, decided to give up. She had a lot of riding ahead of her that day, plus she had to help out with the rally. She couldn't try to help someone who didn't want to be helped. Walking away, she hoped the other Mendenhall riders were nicer than Kurt.

STEVIE STACKED THE paper cups on the table. On one side of the show ring, Mrs. Reg had set up a table with coolers of juice and water. She had also baked a few plates of cookies, and parents of riders contributed some snacks, too. Stevie loved jobs that involved food—Mrs. Reg usually rewarded her with a handful of sweets, and Stevie's stomach didn't seem to mind peanut butter cookies at ten in the morning.

After helping Mrs. Reg, Stevie headed toward the driveway. As she walked by the indoor ring, she glanced inside. A girl was emerging from the stabling area to warm up a horse. It was a familiar sight—the partnership between horse and rider. Horses always needed a chance to warm up before the difficult and stressful act of performing competitively, especially in something as demanding as dressage.

The rider took her horse around the ring at a walk. She asked her horse to lengthen his strides for the second round and then took him to a trot. He responded instantly to her aids, his muscular flanks gleaming. What a beautiful horse he was! The same pretty, rich brown as Carole's horse, Starlight, with Starlight's proud, nearly prancing trot and his famously smooth canter. This horse's ears perked and flicked the same way Starlight's did, too, and—Stevie blinked once, then blinked again to make sure she was seeing things correctly. This horse had a star on his face, too, just like Starlight! And then she noticed that he had three white socks, just like Starlight!

What was that strange girl doing riding Starlight?

4

STEVIE COULD HARDLY believe her eyes. Carole almost always took care of her horse herself. She loved warming up Starlight for competitions, and it wasn't like her to hand the job to a stranger. Something was definitely fishy.

The girl continued to ride Starlight, and Stevie decided to take action. She walked into the indoor ring and began gently waving to the girl. She didn't want to startle the girl or the horse, since both were obviously concentrating on their warm-up. After a few seconds, the girl noticed Stevie and rode over to her. "Can I help you?" she inquired politely.

Without any introduction, Stevie plunged in. "What are you doing with Carole's horse?" she asked.

The girl looked startled. "Carole who?" she asked.

"Carole Hanson, that's who," said Stevie. "One of the best riders I know, one of my best friends, and by the way, that's her horse that you're sitting on."

The girl looked even more puzzled. "No, it's not," she said indignantly. "This is my horse, Indy."

Stevie was about to fire off another accusation, but then she took a closer look at the horse. Although the horse could have been Starlight's twin, he was slightly bulkier and his coat was perhaps a shade lighter. Plus, there were other small differences that Stevie hadn't noticed from far away, like that his mane wasn't braided as well as Starlight's. Her eyes had deceived her. It wasn't Starlight after all.

Stevie was embarrassed. "Uh, I'm sorry," she said to the girl. "I was wrong. Although you'll forgive me as soon as you see Starlight! You would *not* believe how much your horse looks like my friend's horse!"

The girl smiled. She was small like Lisa, but instead of being fine-boned and petite, she was downright skinny. She had a sprinkling of freckles across her nose to go with her sandy hair. "That's okay," she told Stevie. "I forgive you already." She stuck out her hand. "My name's Mo— short for Maureen. I'm from Mendenhall Stables."

"Welcome to Pine Hollow, Mo," said Stevie, shaking her hand. She patted Indy's nose as a welcome, too. "I'm Stevie. Listen, once again, I'm really sorry for my mistake. Now I've just got to find my friend Carole and get her to see your horse!" She hurried off.

When Stevie got to the driveway, Carole, Lisa, and Phil were helping two more Mendenhall riders with their horses. One was a very pretty girl with strawberry blond hair and blue eyes. Her horse was a gorgeous palomino. The other rider was a somewhat gangly boy, with hunched shoulders and bony wrists poking out of his riding jacket. His horse was light gray.

"Carole, you've got to come and see—" Stevie began, but Carole held up a hand to hush her. She was talking to the two riders, telling them where visiting Pony Clubs should go. Stevie waited impatiently until Carole turned to her.

"Stevie, this is Celeste and Howard, from Mendenhall," she said, pointing to the girl and the boy. From the tone of Carole's voice, which was flatly polite and uninterested, Stevie could tell that she didn't think much of either Celeste or Howard. A few seconds later, Stevie found out why.

"Celeste, is there anything else I can do for you right now?" Howard asked eagerly. His voice was high and nasal—definitely a nerd, decided Stevie—and the expression on his face was adoring as he gazed at Celeste.

Celeste looked disdainfully at Howard, then opened her mouth and daintily extracted a wad of gum. "You can throw out my gum for me," she said with icy sweetness.

Howard reverently took the wad of gum from her, and Celeste turned and walked toward the stable.

"I guess I'm taking her horse to the ring for her," muttered Lisa. She picked up the palomino's lead rein.

"You're welcome!" Stevie called out jokingly after Celeste. Celeste didn't appear to hear.

Howard handed the reins of his horse to Carole. Then he carefully removed a handkerchief from his jacket pocket, laid Celeste's gum in the handkerchief, folded it, and replaced it in his pocket.

Phil made a gagging sound, which he quickly turned into a cough. Carole, Lisa, and Stevie all gaped at Howard.

"I bet he's got a collection, and he calls it 'My Favorite Pieces of Gum Chewed by Celeste,'" whispered Stevie.

"Isn't that highly unsanitary?" Carole added, also in a whisper. She was completely amazed at Howard's sickening devotion to Celeste.

Howard bustled importantly over to Lisa, who was still holding the reins of the palomino horse. "Give me those reins," he commanded in a prissy tone. "I'm the only person whom Celeste trusts with Gold Rush."

"Fine with me," Lisa said, nettled, as she handed over the reins. "But who's going to lead your horse?"

Howard hurried away with Gold Rush. "Oh, you can

follow me with my horse. His name is Ghost," he said over his shoulder.

Carole began walking toward the indoor ring with Ghost. She didn't mind taking care of other people's horses if she had time. As she often joked, she'd never met a horse she didn't like, and Ghost was a real beauty, with a silky gray coat and a mane and tail that were almost silver.

"I think Howard is going to end up following *us*," she said dryly. "Just about now, he's going to realize that he has no clue where he's going."

"Oh, Celeste! Can I please kiss the ground you walk on!" Phil said, imitating Howard's nasal whine. Everyone laughed.

"I have to say, I'm not crazy about the Mendenhall riders so far," Lisa commented. "I haven't met a single nice person from that club."

"I have," Stevie said. "Her name is Mo, and she's the reason I came to find you guys in the first place. Or rather, her horse is the reason I came to find you guys. Oh, never mind. Just wait till you see her horse, Carole! You're not going to believe your eyes!"

"What is it?" Carole asked, alarmed. "Is it weird-looking? Does it need my help?"

"Just wait and see," Stevie answered mysteriously.

As the group walked quickly toward the indoor ring,

they noticed Denise and Red huddled near the doorway. They were talking quietly, but it was obvious from their gestures that something was wrong. Denise looked even more upset and distracted than she had all week, and Red seemed worried.

Lisa slowed her steps. "I wonder what's wrong," she said.

Stevie slowed down, too. "Maybe we should stop to find out," she suggested.

Just then, Ghost snorted and pulled at his lead. He was obviously feeling frisky after his long van ride, and Carole spoke to him gently and patted his nose. "Let's keep going," she said. "Ghost needs some exercise to work out these travel kinks. And besides, it could just be a lovers' quarrel. I'm sure Denise and Red don't want us butting in to their business."

"Why not?" Stevie demanded. "We're so helpful. We give such good advice."

"Girls!" groaned Phil. "Always trying to fix things. Let's leave them alone."

As THE GROUP entered the indoor ring, Mo was tying Indy to the fence. When Carole caught sight of Indy, she was shocked. "Hey! What the . . . !" She paused and then understood both her mistake and what Stevie had wanted her to see. "He looks so much like Starlight!" she exclaimed.

"That's what I thought, too," Stevie said triumphantly. "Isn't it amazing? Maybe they're really secret twins! Maybe," she continued dramatically, "Starlight and Indy were separated at birth by cruel people, who forced them to live apart until the day they accidentally met . . ."

"No, Starlight wasn't a twin," said Carole, shaking her head. She knew how Stevie's imagination could go on . . . and on. "It's just an incredible likeness."

The group walked to Mo and Indy. Stevie quickly made the introductions while Carole patted her horse's near twin. Indy even liked to be scratched on the cheek, Starlight's favorite place.

"I'm curious to meet Indy's double," said Mo, smiling at Carole.

"We'll show you," offered Lisa. Mo was just as friendly as Stevie had said. After her unpleasant encounters with Kurt, Celeste, and Howard, Lisa was relieved to finally meet a rider from Mendenhall that she liked.

Mo made sure that Indy was hitched securely to the fence. Then she double-checked her gleaming, carefully polished show tack, which was slung over a bench just outside the ring. She was ready.

The young riders made their way into the stable, Carole in the lead, Mo walking beside her. "Indy's sixteen hands. How tall is Starlight?"

"The same," said Carole. "What's Indy's favorite snack?"

"Apples," said Mo.

"Granny Smith?" Carole asked. Mo nodded. "Starlight's, too." This was getting weird!

When Mo saw Starlight, her jaw dropped. "You weren't kidding!" she said. She scratched him on the cheek and laughed when his ears flicked forward like Indy's.

After visiting Starlight, the group returned to the indoor ring. "I just can't believe it," Mo repeated for the fourth time. "I just can't believe how much Starlight looks like Indy."

"Or how much Indy looks like Starlight," Carole said teasingly. "I can't believe it, either."

"Good thing you don't ride at the same stable," joked Stevie. "It would be like wearing the same outfit as the other person all the time."

Everyone laughed. "I sure hope Starlight and Indy don't feel that way, especially since I spent hours cleaning his tack last—" Mo stopped suddenly, staring just beyond her horse. Her newfound friends stopped just as suddenly.

"Oh no!" Mo exclaimed. Stevie, Lisa, Carole, and Phil looked where she pointed. Indy's shiny clean show tack lay in a tumbled heap on the dusty floor!

"I SPENT HOURS polishing that tack last night!" wailed Mo. She picked up her bridle and tried untangling the reins. All her tack was covered with a fine layer of gritty dust. Someone had even seen fit to put a muddy footprint on Mo's saddle.

The Saddle Club was shocked. "Who would do something so mean?" Lisa wondered aloud.

Mo looked grim. "Celeste and Howard, that's who," she said. "Celeste will do anything—*anything*—to win in competition, and Howard will do anything Celeste asks him to do. Have you met them? They're totally awful."

"Well, they *were* pretty awful when we met them," admitted Carole. "But would they deliberately sabotage someone else's equipment?" Even though she had disliked Celeste and Howard, she couldn't believe they would stoop so low to win a ribbon.

"Yes," answered Mo. "You just don't know them like I do. They've done horrible things to me. This is actually minor compared to some of the stuff they've done. But what am I going to do about my tack?" Her eyes looked suspiciously bright, and The Saddle Club could tell she was on the verge of tears. The dressage rally was due to begin in about forty-five minutes, and it usually took at least that long to get tack into show condition.

Stevie stepped forward. "C'mon, we'll take it to the tack room and help you polish it again. With all of us working, it shouldn't take more than fifteen minutes."

"You'd help me clean my tack?" Mo asked in disbelief.

"Well, I certainly couldn't let Starlight's twin go into the ring looking like that," Carole said, leading the way to the saddle soap.

When they got to the tack room, they found Celeste and Howard putting a few finishing touches on Celeste's tack. Or rather, Howard was working on Celeste's tack. Celeste herself was sitting on a stool, giving Howard directions in her icy-sweet voice. She was swinging her riding crop lightly, using it as a pointer to direct Howard to spots he had missed.

Mo stood in front of the pair and put her hands on her

hips. "You've done some nasty things to win, Celeste, but this is the final straw! How dare you throw my tack onto the floor?"

"Why, whatever are you talking about?" Celeste asked sweetly. Howard didn't say anything. He just shook his head and continued to polish Celeste's saddle.

The Saddle Club was astounded. Celeste was obviously guilty. "I can't believe you would be so mean," Stevie said, glaring at Celeste and Howard. She was always the first person to jump into a fight, and her temper was heating up. Mo was by far the nicest person from Mendenhall, and she was clearly the victim in this case. Carole and Lisa didn't say anything. Even though they were also appalled, they felt uneasy about getting involved in such an ugly situation.

"Maybe you don't know the whole story," suggested a quiet voice from the corner. It was Kurt, who was slowly polishing a pair of stirrups. No one had noticed him before, and after giving him one angry glance, Mo turned her attention back to Celeste and Howard.

"What's there to know? I left my tack in perfect condition and five minutes later it was on the ground," fumed Mo. "I know you two did it. I just know it!"

"Why would I need to damage your tack?" Celeste asked smugly. "I'm a good enough rider to beat you any day."

"I'll tell the officials," Mo threatened, her voice tightening into an infuriated squeak. Celeste's coolness seemed to be angering her even more. "You can't beat me if you aren't allowed in the competition."

Howard stood up and raised a bony hand, attempting to look dignified. "Now, Mo, I don't think you should make a scene," he said pompously.

Stevie chimed in again. "You should be barred from competition," she said loudly to Celeste. "Better yet, you should be barred from all riding stables in the area! This goes beyond bad sportsmanship. You—"

"What's going on here?" Max's voice broke in. The group turned and saw Max and Denise standing in the door of the tack room.

Then Veronica poked her head in the other door. "You're upsetting Danny before the competition. I'll bet you're doing it on purpose. What's all the noise?" she demanded.

"What a busybody," muttered Carole to Lisa.

"Everyone, in my office, *now*," commanded Max. Everyone, even Kurt and Veronica, obeyed immediately. No one argued with Max when he spoke in that tone.

Once they were all in his office, Max shut the door and turned to face the entire group. Denise stood off to the side, also looking stern.

"Now, will someone please tell me what's going on?" Max asked. He looked at Stevie. Obviously, he had heard Stevie's voice arguing loudly along with the rest.

Stevie fidgeted. She hated to be the one to tell on Celeste and Howard. But the memory of what they had done to Mo's tack still rankled, and she couldn't keep silent. Besides, maybe Max could do something about the way Celeste and Howard treated Mo. "Well, you see, Celeste—" she began.

"I am very sorry," Celeste interrupted sweetly. She stepped forward and smiled at Max. "We apologize for making so much noise, don't we, Howard?"

Howard nodded. "Yes, we're sorry."

Stevie was shocked. They were going to try to get away with the whole thing! Outraged, she turned to Mo, waiting for her to tell the dreadful story about her tack. But Mo didn't say a word. So Stevie began again to tell the story. "Mo left her—*Ow!*" Mo nudged Stevie with her elbow, hard. Stevie knew a hint when she felt one. She stared at Mo, saw an icy look on her face, and stopped talking. Carole and Lisa also noticed Mo's nudge and looked at each other in puzzlement.

Stevie found Mo's sudden reticence disturbing. Although she and her friends weren't generally tattlers when riders misbehaved or made mistakes, Celeste's behavior was outrageous and deserved some sort of punishment. Stevie gagged on her own words, then tried to clear her throat. Mo nudged her again, this time even harder.

Stevie lost her balance and stumbled against a nearby

table stacked high with catalogs of horse-related equipment, tack, and riding clothes—all of which cascaded to the floor. As she bent to retrieve them, she noticed a bulging envelope lying haphazardly on the rag rug. She picked it up and saw that it was full of cash.

"Max, what's this?" she said, straightening up and holding out the envelope.

Max turned pale. "Thank you, Stevie," he said, taking the envelope. "That's the refund from the feed company that delivered the bad hay. I must have dropped it—I can't believe I could be so careless." He checked to make sure that none of the bills had dropped out, then put the envelope on a high shelf. He tucked it far behind a stack of books so that it was hidden from view.

Carole, Lisa, and Stevie noticed that the money jar for CARL was also sitting on the shelf and was almost full of change and bills. It looked like Pine Hollow had come up with a substantial donation. After hiding the envelope, Max also pushed the CARL jar behind the stack of books.

Max turned back to the group. "I don't know what's going on here, and none of you seems willing to tell me," he began, fixing each student with a stern eye. "But no matter what a rider's personal feelings are, he or she should never display the type of behavior I saw in the tack room. Part of being a rider is how you carry yourself. It's really important—"

Just then Red stuck his head in the office. "Max, riders from Ballard Hills and more riders from Cross County," he announced.

"Okay, we'll be right there," Max answered, and Denise hurried out. Max looked at the group of riders again and said, "You're spared the lecture, so for the time being, just stay out of trouble and behave yourselves. Now, I'm sure everyone has some preparation to do before the rally, and if not, then try to help other riders. Get started!" With that, Max hurried after Denise. Celeste, Howard, and Kurt followed quickly. Veronica disappeared before anyone could give her a job to do.

Carole and Lisa went up to Mo, who still looked mad. "Let's get that tack clean now," Carole said.

"Thanks," answered Mo in a subdued tone. At the mention of her tack, she began to look less angry and more discouraged. Carole and Lisa couldn't help feeling sorry for her. It was obvious that Celeste often picked on Mo, and they wondered how Mo could stand it. Even though they had to put up with Veronica's pettiness sometimes, it was nothing compared to the obvious bad feeling between Mo and Celeste and Howard.

"Mo, why don't you tell someone about how mean Celeste is to you?" Lisa asked gently.

"What good would it do?" Mo muttered, almost to herself. Then she shrugged. "Thanks for helping me

51

with the tack," she said, walking out of the office. Carole and Lisa looked at each other. It was obvious that Mo didn't want to talk about it, and they didn't know her well enough to pry. They followed her into the tack room.

Veronica was picking up a cloth when they got there. "I can't believe that I was forced to endure that little lecture," she complained to no one in particular. "It had absolutely nothing to do with me, and I have so much to do for Danny before the rally starts."

Stevie and Phil exchanged glances. Red or Denise almost always tacked up Danny for Veronica. They knew that in all likelihood Veronica was bringing the polishing cloth for someone else to do the work. All she had to do, usually, was climb on the horse. "Maybe you weren't caught yelling this time, but otherwise, I'd say you deserve the title of Queen of Screech," said Phil.

"I've had enough of your little remarks, Phil Marsten," Veronica hissed. "You'd better watch your back. And that includes you, little girlfriend!" she added, turning to Stevie. She stomped out, whipping the polishing cloth behind her for effect.

Stevie made a cross with her fingers as if to ward off evil. "Listen, you've had some fun with Veronica, but let's just stay out of her way," she suggested to Phil. "It's the day of our anniversary celebration, remember? And we've got a rally ahead of us.

"Besides," she said as she linked arms with Phil, "I don't know what Veronica meant by 'little.' I'm taller than she is."

6

"There," Lisa said, tightening Prancer's girth. "You're ready to go." Prancer was tacked up and in perfect show form. Her mane and tail were beautifully braided—thanks to Stevie—and Lisa had carefully touched up Prancer's tack after helping Mo with hers.

Prancer turned her head and reached her nose out to Lisa. "Hey," Lisa said, jerking back. Prancer had just nibbled her hair for the fourth or fifth time since she had entered the stall. The horse had also butted Lisa with her head several times.

Lisa shook her head in confusion. Nibbling hair and bumping people playfully was something that Belle, Stevie's horse, was prone to do, but Prancer was usually

54

gentle and more dignified. What had gotten into the mare lately?

Stevie stuck her head over the stall door. "Almost ready?" she asked.

"Yes," answered Lisa. "But I can't get over it. Prancer's still not acting like herself."

"Maybe she's been taken over by body-snatching aliens. The kind of aliens that prefer horses to people. Come to think about it, we should get to know those aliens!" joked Stevie.

Lisa didn't laugh. Normally she found Stevie's dumb jokes at least mildly funny, but Prancer's unexplained behavior was worrying her. It wasn't that she was sick or even naughty, just un-Prancer-like.

A FEW MINUTES later Carole, Lisa, Stevie, Phil, and A.J. met outside and began walking toward the show ring. The rally was due to begin in less than fifteen minutes. Lisa was leading Prancer, since she was one of the first riders scheduled to compete.

Just as they reached the show ring, Max appeared. He looked upset and almost rushed by the girls without seeing them.

"Hey, Max, is something wrong?" Carole called out in concern.

Max halted and looked around. He raked his fingers

through his hair. "The money's gone—all of it. It was in my office ten minutes ago—well, you saw it—and now it's gone! I thought the feed refund and the CARL jar would be safer in the house, so I went back to get it and it was gone!"

"How much money is missing?" asked Phil.

"Over five hundred dollars," Max said glumly.

The Saddle Club could hardly believe their ears. Five hundred dollars! How could that be? They'd all just seen it, and now . . . Who would take five hundred dollars?

Max began looking around. Riders from the different Pony Clubs were beginning to gather with their horses outside the show ring. Parents and other spectators occupied the bleachers just outside the show ring. "I guess I should make an announcement," he said reluctantly. "Maybe someone knows something about the missing money."

Max went to the table at the side of the show ring, where he sat with the judges. He raised his hand and the crowd quieted down. Usually Max opened shows at Pine Hollow with a welcoming greeting for all the visiting Pony Clubs. Today his first remarks had quite a different tone.

"I have a very disturbing announcement to make," began Max. He didn't look worried and upset anymore. Carole, Lisa, and Stevie knew that in a crisis Max usually managed to maintain a rational and calm appearance.

"Someone has just taken a large sum of money out of my office."

The crowd began to murmur. Max held up his hand for silence. "It was my fault for being so careless as to leave it there, but I've always encouraged an open atmosphere at this stable and I didn't think it would be a problem. Now the money is gone, and if anyone knows anything about the disappearance, please come and talk to me. If you know where the money is, you can just leave it in my office when I'm not there—no questions asked."

The riders from visiting Pony Clubs shuffled uneasily, and several people darted glances at each other. Then Veronica diAngelo stepped forward. "I know something," she said, looking pleased with herself.

"Uh-oh," whispered Stevie. Veronica had an expression on her face that meant trouble. But even Stevie didn't anticipate what Veronica said next.

"I know who took the money," announced Veronica. "Phil Marsten is the thief. I saw him sneaking out of your office ten minutes ago!"

VERONICA'S ACCUSATION SET off a shock wave of reaction. Stevie could hardly believe her ears. Had Veronica lost her mind? Maybe she was still mad at Phil because of all his teasing, but this was too much!

Members of the Cross County Pony Club, who were all good friends with Phil, began protesting his innocence. "That's a lie, Veronica!" A.J. called out. Phil's parents looked outraged at Veronica's words. Members of other Pony Clubs who didn't know Phil began craning their necks for a glimpse of the supposed thief.

Stevie opened her mouth to tell Veronica off, but Max forestalled her. "No, Stevie. Let Phil speak," he ordered.

An uneasy silence fell over the group. Phil looked around uncomfortably and then glanced at Veronica, his green eyes cold. "That's ridiculous!" he said. "I didn't take the money. I haven't had any money for weeks—I'm always broke," he added, trying to make a joke of it. The joke fell flat, and no one laughed.

Stevie turned and faced Veronica. "You can't just make crazy accusations like that in front of all these people!" She was so mad her voice shook. "Who do you think you are?"

Veronica didn't look the least bit ashamed. In fact, Stevie had never seen her look so sure of herself. "I'm only reporting what I saw with my own eyes," she answered smugly. "I have proof that Phil Marsten is the thief. I saw him skulking around Max's office. He looked so guilty, I knew he was up to something."

"There's only one explanation for this," Stevie said sarcastically. "Either you need a pair of glasses, or you're completely off your rocker. You didn't see *anything*, did you? You're just making it up." Then she looked at Phil, expecting him to deny Veronica's statement. To her dismay, Phil had turned red. "Phil, tell her the truth," she pleaded.

Phil turned even redder and wouldn't meet her eyes. "I did go into Max's office about ten minutes ago," he admitted.

"Why?" Stevie asked, bewildered.

"Just because," mumbled Phil. "But," he added defiantly, "I didn't take the money."

No one knew how to react at first. Phil was acting very strangely, completely unlike his usual frank, open self. He didn't seem to want to volunteer any more information.

"If Phil says he didn't do it, that's good enough for me," A.J. said at last, looking around. "I believe him."

Max looked at Phil thoughtfully. He knew Phil almost as well as he knew Stevie, and he had always liked and trusted him. "I'll take your word for it, Phil," he said. "Let's try to figure this out later. We should go on with the rally as planned. We'll start a little later, though—in fifteen minutes. I'm going to search the office one more time." He hurried off.

Phil smiled at Stevie, but his smile looked uncertain compared to his usual grin. He walked off with A.J. for a last-minute Cross County pep talk.

"Gosh," a voice said. "He looks too nice to be a thief."

The Saddle Club turned to see Mo, standing with Indy. "He *is* too nice to be a thief," said Stevie. "He didn't do it!"

"Are you sure?" Mo asked gently. "I mean, I know he's your boyfriend, but that dark-haired girl saw him sneaking around the office. And no one else saw anything. If he didn't take the money, what was he doing?"

"I'm sure there's a perfectly logical explanation for what Phil was doing," said Stevie, getting heated again. She was starting to not like Mo quite so much anymore.

Then she stopped and thought for a second. From an

outsider's point of view, Phil did look sort of guilty. But Stevie knew it was absolutely out of the question that Phil Marsten would take a dime, much less five hundred dollars. On the other hand, he had turned bright red when Veronica accused him of sneaking around Max's office, and he hadn't denied that part at all. Nor had he explained what he was doing there. But Stevie knew that that just meant he was up to something, not that he was a thief!

Carole and Lisa, thinking along the same lines, were also wondering why Phil hadn't explained his presence in Max's office. But they didn't say so in front of Mo. They liked Phil a lot, and they'd never question his motives in front of a stranger. "Phil's one of the most honest people we know," Lisa told her.

"Yes, and one of the most trustworthy," agreed Carole.

Stevie looked gratefully at her two friends. Then, as Mo walked off, she whispered, "Saddle Club emergency meeting—right now!"

Lisa hitched Prancer to a post and they all hurried off to a quiet spot under a tree. Stevie, wasting no time, started complaining about Veronica. "She's just pulling one of her awful stunts, only this one is even more under-handed than most," she said angrily. "She's just getting even with Phil for his jokes about her."

"Maybe so, but that doesn't solve the crime," Lisa said sensibly. Stevie shot her a dirty glance. Sometimes she wished that Lisa weren't quite so logical. "I mean," Lisa added meekly, "the only way to clear Phil's name after a public accusation like that is to find the real thief."

"Lisa's right," said Carole. "And besides, we should try to clear this up for Max, too. He's feeling really bad about leaving that money in his office, and I don't want him thinking that he can't invite riders to come here anymore. Pine Hollow has always been a place where you can leave doors open and not worry about a thing. We don't lock our cubbies, do we? I would hate to see that openness and trust change. I would hate for us all to start suspecting one another of stealing things."

Stevie saw Carole's point. Pine Hollow was a special sort of place, and everyone—including Veronica, who often left expensive things lying around—seemed to trust one another. But she was still mad. "I bet Veronica stole that money herself just so she could point the finger at Phil!" she declared.

"I don't know, Stevie," Carole said reluctantly. "Veronica did seem to be telling the truth about seeing Phil come out of the office. She looked so sure of herself when she said that, and she isn't that good of a liar."

Stevie glowered at Carole. "What are you saying? That you think Phil did it?" she demanded.

"Of course not," Carole said hastily. "I'm just saying that we have to keep all possibilities open, that Veronica may not be the answer. We should try to find the real thief for Phil's sake."

"Yes, and for Max's, too," said Lisa.

TEN MINUTES LATER, the first round of the dressage rally was announced. There were to be four rounds of tests, exactly like the first four levels of actual dressage tests. The first level involved basic dressage movements, like fifteen- and ten-meter circles, lengthening of the stride, serpentines, leg yields, and counter-canters.

Carole had left the group and headed back to the stable to get Starlight for her turn. She paused by the fence to watch Mo, who was one of the first riders to perform. She saw the owner and riding instructor from Mendenhall reach up and shake Mo's hand to wish her luck.

"He looks like a nice man," Carole said to herself. The owner was tall and looked several years older than Max, with graying hair and a nice smile. Then Mo's name was announced, and she and Indy began the first test. The ring became absolutely quiet. Show events usually took place in silence, with applause only at the end of each rider's turn. Riders and horses needed total concentration, and the parents and spectators at the rally knew that. When Carole had first started competing in events, she had trained her father not to cheer until she had finished riding. She could see her dad now, sitting in the stands and watching intently.

Mo finished the serpentine. "She's good," Carole said to herself. Since Carole was the best rider at Pine Hollow, she was a pretty good judge of riding ability. She could tell that Mo had practiced a lot of dressage before. Indy moved smoothly into different steps without any visible aids from Mo.

Watching Indy, Carole still could not get over the resemblance between him and Starlight. She knew Starlight so well that she would never confuse him with Indy, as Stevie had, even from a distance. Still, the resemblance was uncanny.

LISA WAITED BY the fence with Prancer. Her turn for the first round was coming up soon. Near her, Celeste waited with Gold Rush and Howard waited with Ghost.

As much as Lisa disliked Celeste, she had to admit that Celeste and Gold Rush made a striking combination. Gold Rush's creamy mane and tail were perfectly braided—Lisa was sure Howard had something to do with that—and Celeste herself was beautifully dressed, with her strawberry blond hair tucked into a tight braid. Her blue eyes looked determined and cold.

Looking at Celeste, Lisa was reminded of something Stevie had said once. Stevie was telling one of her funny stories and describing the expression on her brothers' faces when they were getting ready for big soccer games. "They call it their game face," Stevie had said. "Their faces start looking like this," and she had set her face into grim, tight lines. Carole and Lisa had giggled—Stevie looked as if she were in pain. "Well, the idea is that they are determined to win and don't want to show any kindness or humanity or even personality to the other guys. It's as if a smile would be giving something away to the opponents," she had explained.

Lisa thought she knew now what Stevie had meant by "game face." If ever someone had on a game face, it was Celeste.

Next to Celeste, Howard was murmuring reassuringly. "You'll win," Lisa heard him saying. "No one here can even come close to you as a rider." His own game face was an adoring stare at the girl who barely acknowledged his existence.

Lisa knew it was wrong to eavesdrop, but she was curious about Celeste and Howard. She wanted to know more about their odd relationship; and besides, she needed to keep her eyes and ears open if she was going to solve the theft. Besides, she could practically hear everything they were saying, anyway. If she could just get a little closer . . .

Trying to look unobtrusive, Lisa edged toward Celeste and Howard. Howard continued to murmur encouraging words to Celeste.

"You have iron nerves," he was saying. "You look completely together, and we all know that poise is half the battle in dressage. I'm actually feeling a little nervous, what with the theft and all. It's disgraceful, how this stable is run! I really think someone should speak to the owner about security here. If there's a thief on the loose, nothing is safe. In fact, I think all the riders are feeling unsettled after that little incident."

"Good," Celeste answered coolly. "I hope you're right, Howard. I hope everyone's confidence is shaken, because that gives me an even better chance of winning!"

Lisa's eyes widened. Celeste was even worse than she'd thought. Talk about poor sportsmanship! Why, she even sounded glad that the money was gone. Like, really glad. That made Lisa pause. Just how glad *was* Celeste? Could Celeste be the thief? Had she taken the money just to rattle everyone else?

AFTER LEAVING THE Saddle Club meeting, Stevie searched for Phil. She found him talking to A.J. about the upcoming round. Stevie didn't waste time on politeness. She dragged Phil away without any explanation and got him alone near the stable. "What's the deal?" she asked bluntly. "What were you doing around Max's office?"

Phil looked around, trying to act casual. "I was just hanging around."

"Look here, Phil," Stevie said impatiently. "I don't believe for a second that you're guilty, but I need your help!

Carole, Lisa, and I have made up our minds—we're going to find the real thief so that we can clear your name."

Phil looked pleased. "Hey, that's really great of you—"

"Hold the gratitude," interrupted Stevie. "Now, why were you in Max's office?"

"I don't remember why I went into Max's office," answered Phil. Then he snapped his fingers. "Oh yeah! I needed something from the tack room and I just went into Max's office by mistake."

Stevie sighed. Phil had visited Pine Hollow many times before, and it was very unlikely that he would make a mistake like that—even if he was distracted by the upcoming rally. She was getting more and more frustrated. Why was Phil lying to her? He didn't even seem bothered by the fact that a lot of people thought he was a thief.

Stevie had known Phil for a long time, and if there was one thing she knew, it was that Phil was trustworthy. Even though they had squabbled a lot over who was a better rider, she had never had any reason to doubt his honesty. So why wasn't he telling her the truth now?

Just then Denise ran past, bumping into Stevie by accident. "Oh, sorry," she mumbled, and continued on her way.

In the corner of her mind, Stevie noticed that Denise was still looking worried and distracted. In fact, she was completely unlike her usual calm, capable self. *Her school and workloads must really be getting to her*, Stevie thought. She made a mental note to remind her friends to be helpful to Denise. Then she turned her attention back to her number one concern.

She decided to try one more time to wheedle the information out of Phil. "Phil, think about it," she coaxed. "I mean, *really* think about how Veronica's accusation made you look. Do you want everyone—besides me, Carole, and Lisa and your friends at Cross County—walking around thinking you're a thief?"

"No, of course not," said Phil. He looked angry at the idea that other people suspected him.

Feeling more hopeful, Stevie continued, "So don't you think we should find the thief?"

"Of course," said Phil. "Not just for me, but for Max. He lost an awful lot of money."

"So we need to explain what you were doing in Max's office," said Stevie. "Otherwise, it looks strange, you going in there so close to the time of the theft."

Phil leaned forward and gave Stevie a quick kiss on the cheek. "I've got to go check on Teddy," he said. "Good luck in the first round." He tweaked her nose, winked at her, and hurried off, leaving her more frustrated than ever.

I'll get it out of him somehow, she thought.

THE FIRST ROUND of the dressage rally was over. Stevie had been one of the final riders to go, and although she and Belle had performed well, she hadn't been able to concentrate as much as she normally did. It had taken her longer than usual to get Belle to lengthen her strides, and her circles had been a bit wobbly. Stevie could feel the mare's confusion at her occasional inattention. Normally, anything less than a perfect dressage performance would have thrown Stevie into a pit of despair, but right now she was too worried about the theft.

Carole had competed right after Stevie. She and Starlight turned in a beautiful round. Carole let hardly anything affect her riding, even though dressage wasn't a craze with her the way it was with Stevie.

After taking care of their horses, the two girls met up with Lisa, who was waiting for them near the refreshment table. When the first round had ended, the area around the show ring had become crowded with parents and spectators who were taking advantage of the break to stretch their legs. The sun was getting higher in the sky, and Pine Hollow was taking on a relaxed, picniclike atmosphere. On any other day, the girls would have been loving every minute of the rally.

They saw their parents near the refreshment table, drinking juice and munching cookies. "I hope my dad doesn't eat *all* the oatmeal cookies," Carole said when she saw him. "I usually stop him after four or five."

Lisa giggled at Carole's maternal tone. She knew that her friend often acted like that because her mother had died a few years before. Carole helped her father with housework and often fussed over whether he was eating healthy foods or dating the right women.

Stevie didn't appear to hear either Carole or Lisa. She was looking around impatiently, and her friends knew she was worrying about solving the theft. "We need privacy," muttered Stevie. She grabbed Carole and Lisa each by the arm and dragged them through the crowd. They finally found a quiet spot near Max's house.

"Now, look," Stevie began in a businesslike voice. "We have a half hour before the second round of the rally, and all of us are scheduled to go late in the round. That gives us a little time to investigate the crime before our turns. Then we have the lunch break before the final two rounds, and we'll use that time to give each other updates on what we found out. Now let's really get down to business. Who had the best motive for taking the money? Who's on our list of suspects? I, for one, still put my money on Veronica."

"I've been thinking," said Lisa. "The person who took the money must have been in the room when Max was lecturing us about proper behavior. Remember? We were all dragged in there and then Stevie found the money on the floor and Max put it up on the shelf with the CARL jar."

"Lots of people go in and out of that office," said Carole. "It could have been anyone."

"No, Lisa's right," Stevie said thoughtfully. "When Max put that money away, he shoved it far behind those books. He did the same thing with the CARL jar. The people in that room were the only ones who saw him hide the money."

"That really narrows the list of suspects," said Carole. "Especially since you can exclude us."

"And Phil," Stevie reminded her. Carole and Lisa agreed.

"So that leaves Denise, Veronica, Celeste, Howard, Mo, and Kurt. Max doesn't count, of course, because why would he steal from himself?" said Lisa, checking off the names on her fingers.

"You can cross Denise off the list, too," suggested Carole. "She would never do anything like this."

"I agree," Stevie said, but she suddenly looked worried.

"What is it?" Carole asked.

"I just remembered," answered Stevie. "When I was trying to talk to Phil a little while ago, I saw Denise hurry past. She looked awful—white-faced and jittery and really nervous. She bumped into me and barely even noticed. In fact, she's been like that all week—except she looked even worse when I saw her. I thought it was just the stress of the rally getting to her, but now . . ."

The three girls looked at each other. "And she *does* need money for her college tuition," Carole said slowly, voicing the thought in all of their minds. She hated to say it out loud. Denise had been such a good friend to them, but they also couldn't forget how desperate she had looked when talking about her tuition.

"Look," Lisa said reasonably. "We'll just leave her on the list for now because we don't know anything. But I don't really think five hundred dollars would solve Denise's tuition worries." Her friends nodded uneasily.

Stevie changed the subject. "How about Veronica?" she reminded them. "She has the motive—she wants to

get even with Phil for his teasing—and she had the op-
portunity, since she could have easily slipped back into
the office after we helped Mo with her tack."

"She's done worse things before," Carole said quietly.
Veronica's behavior had often gotten herself, her horses,
and The Saddle Club into a lot of trouble.

"So Veronica's on the list as well. What about the
Mendenhall riders?" Lisa said.

"We don't really know anything about them," Carole
said thoughtfully.

"We know that Celeste and Kurt are pretty unpleasant," answered Lisa, "and that Mo thinks Celeste is capable of some awful things."

"Right," said Stevie. "The same Mo who wouldn't give
Max any kind of an explanation about all that yelling, so
now he's annoyed at us!"

"I saw Celeste before her turn in the rally, and she was
looking like she would do anything to win," Lisa said.
She told Carole and Stevie about Celeste's smug satisfac-
tion at the effect of the theft on the other riders.

"That means we can't rule out Howard, either," said
Carole. "We've already seen that Howard will do practically anything for Celeste. Maybe even steal."

Stevie clapped her hands together. "Enough talking—
more action!" she declared. "We've got our suspects, and
now we've got to get that money back for Max and

CARL. We have to investigate people while they're here, now, at the scene of the crime. The trail is still fresh, although it's getting colder by the second. Sooner or later, the guilty party will reveal herself."

Lisa knew that Stevie's "herself" referred to Veronica. When it came to suspecting Veronica of wrongdoing, Stevie had a one-track mind, and she wasn't going to forget Veronica's accusation of Phil anytime soon. Lisa herself wasn't so sure. Her friends hadn't heard Celeste and Howard talking. And everyone had seen the panicked look on Denise's face. Nobody knew anything about Kurt. No, it wasn't a sure thing, much as Stevie wanted it to be. There was work to be done, and Lisa was the one to parcel it out.

"Carole, can you find out what's going on with Denise and Veronica?" she said. "Stevie will take Celeste and Howard while I check out Kurt and Mo. We'll then take our turns in the second round of the rally and report to each other at lunchtime. Same Saddle Club place, same Saddle Club time. Got it?"

Stevie and Carole nodded. Then they all split up and hurried to begin their investigation.

STEVIE LOOKED FOR Celeste and Howard in the indoor ring, where the visiting horses were waiting between rounds. At first she didn't see them, because the ring was pretty crowded. Then she spotted them in the far corner, huddled together and whispering. At least, Howard was huddling and whispering. Celeste appeared to be her usual icy, detached self. She was hard to read because she never seemed to show anything—except perhaps an occasional flicker of contempt for Howard's devotion, which wasn't enough to keep him from waiting on her hand and foot.

Stevie sidled up to them. They definitely looked guilty, she thought. Their heads were close together, and Howard was speaking in low tones and darting furtive glances around him. She wished she could lip-read and understand what they were saying.

If she could just get closer, she might be able to overhear their conversation. Trying to look casual, she picked up a tick of hay and looked for a hungry horse. A bay hitched next to Ghost seemed a likely candidate. Stevie was a few steps away, almost near enough to overhear the pair from Mendenhall, when a loud voice suddenly hailed her. "Hey, Stevie, have you seen Phil?" asked A.J.

Celeste and Howard looked up, startled. Howard looked embarrassed and turned his eyes to the ground. Celeste looked at Stevie, who had gone bright red and looked plainly guilty to be caught so close to them. "Were you spying on us?" she asked angrily.

"Me? Spying? No way!" Stevie said as positively as she

could. "I was just bringing some hay over here for good old, uh, Horse," she said, stumbling for a name and patting the horse's neck. She dropped the tick of hay on top of the pile of hay that was already there. So much for that ruse. Time to try something else.

Stevie took A.J. by the arm. "A.J., do you know where Phil is?" she asked. "I thought I saw him over here, but I guess I was wrong."

A.J. got even more confused as Stevie led him away. "That's what *I* just asked *you*," he reminded her.

"Shhh," hissed Stevie. When she got far enough away from Celeste and Howard, she dashed off, leaving a bewildered A.J. behind.

"Girls," he muttered.

LISA WANDERED THE stable grounds, looking for Kurt. The other riders were also milling around, mingling with each other and the parents who had come to watch. The second round was due to begin in fifteen minutes, and Lisa overheard animated discussion about who had done well in the first round. She passed by the refreshment table and snagged a cookie—lunch seemed far away, and she didn't want to investigate her suspects on a completely empty stomach.

While munching her cookie, Lisa spotted Kurt, standing off by himself underneath a tree. His expression, as usual, was moody and glum. Lisa tried to get closer to

76

him, but she was hampered by the crowd at the refreshment table. After his behavior that morning, she knew he would not be particularly interested in her company—or anyone's company, for that matter.

Just as she got close to the tree, Kurt glanced around and quickly strode off. Lisa followed, trying to look casual as she traced his path but not feeling casual at all. She lost him inside the stable and then searched the tack room, all of the stalls, and even the locker room. Kurt's bay horse, Simon, was standing tethered in the indoor ring with a large stack of hay in front of him, but Kurt was nowhere to be seen. It was as if he had vanished into thin air.

Lisa sighed. She didn't think she was cut out for this spying business. Her first suspect and she had lost him! Plus, she couldn't help feeling irritated that she was doing it. She and Carole and Stevie had really looked forward to the dressage rally, and now they were spending all their time chasing after a thief. She wanted to quit the investigation, but she also wanted to find Max's money and clear Phil's name.

She went to look for her other suspect, Mo, even though she felt foolish doing it. Mo was so nice, it just didn't seem possible that she could be capable of stealing.

She found Mo giving Indy an in-between grooming in a stall.

"Hi," Mo said to Lisa. "Max was nice enough to let me

use some brushes here. He's so great. I wish the owner of Mendenhall was half as nice."

Lisa smiled with pride. Pine Hollow's riders all loved Max, even though he was strict, and it didn't surprise her that Mo recognized what a great person he was. It was hard to believe that someone had stolen from him and, almost worse, from a charity.

"We think Max is great, too," she told Mo. "But don't tell him. We don't want him to get a swelled head."

"Do you need some help with Prancer?" Mo asked eagerly. "I could give you a hand after I finish up here."

Lisa shook her head. "No thanks," she said. "I'm, uh, in the middle of something, so I'm not doing any additional grooming right now. I'll see you later, okay? Good luck with the next round."

"See ya," answered Mo, returning to her task.

As Lisa walked away, she felt relieved. Mo wasn't a thief. She cared for her horse; she liked Max; she was just like Lisa and her friends. Confidently, Lisa crossed Mo's name off the list of suspects.

CAROLE DIDN'T HAVE to look hard to find Veronica. As usual, she was overseeing someone else's work on her horse. Veronica and Denise were in Danny's stall. Denise was working. Veronica was not. This didn't qualify as suspicious, just normal.

Carole didn't mind spying on Veronica. Experience had taught her that Veronica was capable of some pretty rotten acts, so suspecting her in a theft of money that Veronica couldn't possibly need didn't even feel awkward. Suspecting Denise was another thing altogether. Carole swallowed hard to overcome her distaste for the spying she was about to do. Without letting either Veronica or Denise see her, she quietly opened the door to the next stall, which was fortunately empty, and ducked inside.

She heard nothing out of the ordinary. That is, Veronica was complaining, as usual, about something to do with Danny, and Denise was doing all the work.

"Well, you'll just have to braid Danny's mane all over again," Veronica snapped. "Red just didn't do it right the first time."

"Mmmm-hmmm," answered Denise.

Carole was surprised. Even though Denise was always tactful, she was also pretty firm with Veronica. It was unlike her not to defend Red against Veronica's whining.

"I specifically asked Red to bring a light gray yarn for Danny's mane," continued Veronica. "This yarn is *medium* gray. Doesn't he know the difference?"

Again, Denise murmured a noncommittal reply. Carole shook her head in disgust and quietly eased out of the stall. She had discovered nothing except that Denise was still acting weird. And that made Carole feel weird, too. She fervently hoped that her suspicions about Denise were wrong.

9

Lisa led Prancer into her stall. The first half of the dressage rally was over. She, Carole, and Stevie had ridden well in the second round, which involved medium gaits, walk-canter transitions, counter-canters, half-turns on haunches, and other second-level figures. Stevie had managed to put her worries about the investigation aside, and she and Belle had competed beautifully, with grace and precision. The three girls were meeting for lunch to compare notes about their suspects. But first they had to take care of their horses.

Lisa removed Prancer's bridle and gave her some water. She left the saddle on, with the girth loosened, for the afternoon session of the rally. Then she dug into her jacket pocket and held out a fistful of carrot sticks.

"Here, Prancer," she said softly. "I brought some treats for you."

Prancer nosed her fingers, then suddenly gobbled down the carrot sticks, almost nipping Lisa's fingers off in the process. Lisa quickly drew her fingers back. "What is wrong with you?" she asked in dismay. Normally Prancer was a polite horse, with manners that were almost dainty. Now she was butting Lisa with her nose, trying to get more treats.

"I don't have any more," Lisa told Prancer sternly. "Especially not for a horse that acts as greedy as you do. What has gotten into you, Prancer?" The horse, after discovering that Lisa wasn't handing out more carrots, started shifting restlessly and nosing around her stall.

Lisa sighed. She was starting to think that Prancer's behavior was a bigger mystery than who stole the money. She went to join Carole and Stevie.

OUTSIDE WAS A colorful scene. Almost all the families had brought picnic lunches for the lunchtime break, and most of the riders were eating brown-bag lunches with their teams. People were good-naturedly angling for the best picnic spaces, crowding together under shady trees.

The Saddle Club met at their favorite lunchtime spot, the grassy knoll overlooking Pine Hollow's schooling ring and the paddocks beyond. Carole spread out a large blanket to sit on so that they wouldn't get grass stains on their riding breeches.

Stevie waved at her parents and brothers, who were sitting with the Marstens. Phil's parents still looked concerned and upset about the scene earlier that morning, and Stevie hoped her parents could cheer them up. Just thinking about Veronica's accusation made her angry all over again. Why would Veronica say that? Even by Veronica's standards, that was low. Stevie shook her head. She could only hope that Carole or Lisa had learned something that might help.

"I wonder where Phil is," she commented.

"Probably eating with his team," said Carole. "And we would be, too, if it weren't for this theft." The three girls munched their sandwiches in gloomy silence. Then Stevie became all business.

"Time to debrief each other," she announced. "I saw Celeste and Howard together, and they were clearly plotting something. They had their heads together and were whispering. Well, Howard was whispering. She was mostly glaring. But it was definitely a *secretive* glare."

"Did you hear what they were saying?" asked Lisa, taking a bite of her peanut butter sandwich.

"No," admitted Stevie, "but they *looked* really guilty."

"So did Kurt," said Lisa. "Before I could approach him, he ran away. And I couldn't find him anywhere after that."

"Was he running away from you?" Carole asked.

"I don't think he even saw me," Lisa said.

"Guilty!" Stevie declared.

"Look, this is not enough to go on," reasoned Carole, taking a juice box out of her lunch bag. "We need more than someone just looking guilty. We need *proof*."

"Mo was completely normal when I saw her," offered Lisa. "She said some really nice things about Max. I think we can pretty much cross her off the list."

"Not yet," argued Stevie. "Everyone's a suspect—except Phil and us. What did you find out about Veronica?" she asked Carole.

Carole took a long sip of juice before answering. "I listened to Veronica and Denise in Danny's stall," she finally answered. "Veronica was acting like her usual self: spoiled rotten. Denise, though . . ." She paused, reluctant to implicate the instructor.

"Denise what?" Stevie asked impatiently.

"Denise was *definitely* acting weird," admitted Carole. "I mean, Veronica was abusing Red, and Denise just stood there and *took* it from her. That's not like her. She usually gives as good as she gets."

"Better," Stevie said.

"But that doesn't make her guilty," said Lisa.

The three girls continued discussing their investigation. Stevie kept pushing Veronica as the prime suspect.

Lisa thought Kurt might have done it, and all three of them thought Celeste was also a likely candidate.

"Maybe Howard did it for her," suggested Carole again.

"Even if he did, Celeste probably *made* him do it," said Lisa. She couldn't help it—she felt sorry for Howard. He was so pathetic, always hungering after Celeste's approval, while Celeste only tolerated him as her personal servant. Part of her was disgusted at how Howard fawned all over the girl just to get some attention from her, but another part instinctively sensed how weak Howard was and how easily bullied he was by Celeste.

The discussion was interrupted by the appearance of Mo, who was walking up the knoll. "Hi," she called out. "Mind if I join you?"

"*Ixnay* on the *eftthay alktay*," warned Stevie in an undertone. Lisa and Carole nodded in agreement, even though they both felt bad about it. However, technically Mo had not been crossed off their list of suspects.

Mo came up to the group and plopped down on the blanket with a dejected expression. She didn't appear to notice that the conversation had stopped abruptly upon her entrance. "I can't take it another minute," she announced. "Maybe I'll quit riding."

"What is it?" Carole asked, concerned.

Mo bent her head. Her voice trembled as if she was about to cry. "It's Celeste," she told them. "She's been making fun of me again. She just told me that I look like a scarecrow in my riding clothes. I can't help being so skinny. My parents are both skinny; it's inherited."

Lisa patted her shoulder comfortingly. "You look fine in your riding clothes," she said.

"Yes, and you're such a good rider," added Carole. "That's what really counts. Horse shows aren't fashion shows. It's all about who's the best, most skilled rider."

"I know, but *you* know how much appearance counts in dressage," said Mo. "I hate Celeste. She's so competitive, she does anything she can to win. She's totally ruthless, and she has her boy toy, Howard, do everything for her. Not only that, but she's one of the prettiest girls I've ever seen. Everyone at Mendenhall thinks she's pretty, too. You have to admit, that counts sometimes with judges."

"I don't think it does at all," said Carole. The thought that judges would judge on anything other than riding shocked her.

"That's because you're beautiful, too," said Mo. "Celeste is right—I look like a freak in riding clothes."

"I've got a great idea," said Stevie. "Let's start a new Pony Club just for Veronica, Celeste, and Howard. Just think how much fun they could have being obnoxious to one another. And none of them would ever bother us again—except at rallies, but we wouldn't have to invite them!"

"Don't I wish," Mo said. Then she leaned forward and spoke in a whisper. "You have no idea how competitive Celeste *really* is," she told them softly.

The Saddle Club leaned forward to listen.

"A few months ago, one of our riders fell from her horse," continued Mo, still speaking in a low tone, though it wasn't necessary since nobody else was anywhere near them. "She was practicing in the ring, and a loud noise spooked the horse. The rider was badly injured—the horse accidentally trampled her and broke a few of her bones. She was in the hospital for weeks."

"How terrible!" Lisa exclaimed, shuddering. Carole and Stevie looked horrified, too.

"That's not all," said Mo. "I saw Howard running away a few seconds after the accident, and he was carrying a cap pistol. What would he be doing with something like that? The day after the fall, I saw Celeste hugging Howard. Normally she wouldn't be caught dead doing that." Mo paused while the implications of Celeste and Howard's behavior sank in.

"That rider was Celeste's main competition at Mendenhall," she continued. "Now she's out of commission for at least six more months. They're not even sure she'll ever ride again. Celeste's been winning all the local riding events since the accident."

"That's awful," said Stevie angrily. "Why didn't you tell someone? She can't get away with this!"

Mo shrugged. "Who would believe me? Celeste is the star of our Pony Club. The owner of Mendenhall completely dotes on her and listens to everything she says."

"Still, maybe if you said something . . . ," began Lisa, recalling Mo's reluctance to let Stevie tell Max what happened to her tack that morning.

But Mo shook her head again. "Believe me, I've tried," she said positively. "And it hasn't worked. Now I'm worried about what Celeste will do next," she added, looking upset again. "I love Indy with all my heart, and I don't want anything to happen to him or me."

What was Mo saying? Was she actually implying that Celeste would hurt Indy? Carole couldn't imagine what she would do if anything happened to Starlight. She was thankful that Pine Hollow didn't have a rider like Celeste around. Veronica was mean and did some pretty vindictive things, but she wouldn't intentionally do anything to harm a horse or a rider. Ever since her first horse, Cobalt, had died as a result of her own carelessness, Veronica had been a more careful horsewoman. Carole grew sad just thinking about it. Before she had gotten her own horse, she had spent hours taking care of Cobalt, and she still missed him.

She was brought out of her gloom by Stevie's remark. "Pine Hollow is the best stable around," Stevie was saying. "We can't imagine riding anywhere else. All the riders here are really fun people—well, except for Veronica, but she's the only bad apple in the bunch. The rest of us have a great time together, and we talk horses and riding all the time."

"Yes, and Max and Denise are fantastic instructors," Lisa said eagerly. "Red is our head stable hand, and he's terrific, too. I was almost a beginner when I came here, and they've taught me so much."

Amused, Carole realized that Stevie and Lisa had turned to another task at hand—recruiting Mo as a new rider for Pine Hollow! "I'd probably have to tie a red ribbon on Starlight's bridle," she joked, joining the conversation. "Otherwise, I might groom Indy one day by mistake!" Everyone laughed.

Mo looked more cheerful. "Thanks," she said gratefully. "I'd love to join Pine Hollow, but it's an hour away from my house. It would be a long haul for my parents to drive me that far and back."

Lisa became aware of something moving to her left. She flicked her eyes there. It was Kurt. He was looking at the four girls together. He stood motionless for just a second, then his eyes met Lisa's. It was almost a silent plea. He opened his mouth as if to speak, then closed it, hesitated for a second, and shook his head. Lisa blinked. She watched him walking away. What was *with* that boy?

The other girls noticed Lisa's distraction and looked to see what had caught her attention. Kurt's back was to them, and his shoulders were hunched.

"It's like he has a sign on him saying, 'Leave me alone,'" said Carole.

Stevie turned to Mo. "Just what is Kurt's problem, anyway?" she asked, trying to keep her voice casual.

"Kurt's always like that," Mo answered, shrugging. "He's the most antisocial person at Mendenhall. He keeps to himself, doesn't like to talk to anyone."

Lisa nodded. She had experienced that for herself.

"I have heard plenty of rumors about Kurt, though," continued Mo, again dropping her voice to a whisper. "He has two older brothers, both of whom are in jail. I think one of them robbed a store."

"That's so awful for Kurt," said Carole. "Maybe he won't talk to anyone because he's embarrassed about his family."

"It's not just his family," Mo said. "I've heard that Kurt has had his own problems with the police. We go to the same school, and some of my friends told me that he has to report to a probation officer at least once a week."

The Saddle Club members exchanged significant glances. Kurt had gotten into trouble with the police?

"Do you know why?" asked Lisa. "I mean, what did he do?"

"No one knows for sure," said Mo.

"Where there's smoke, there's fire," muttered Stevie. It was a saying that she had heard from Carole's dad. Even if the rumors about Kurt were unconfirmed, why would the rumors exist if there wasn't something shady about his past?

"Huh?" asked Mo, startled.

"Nothing," said Stevie. She spotted Phil coming toward them. "Hey, Phil!" she called out, waving.

Phil walked up to the group, but his eyes were focused on Stevie. "C'mon," he said, grinning. "Let's take a little walk together."

Stevie allowed herself to be pulled up, although she was reluctant to stop discussing the Mendenhall riders. Mo's knowledge was really valuable for the investigation.

Stevie and Phil walked for a few minutes together, discussing the first two rounds of the dressage rally. Stevie wanted to tell him about their investigation, but he seemed distracted and excited about something else. All her attempts to raise the subject failed as he murmured replies like "Is that so?" and "Oh, really?"

"Phil, we're trying to help you and Max and you don't even care," Stevie finally said, exasperated.

They had reached Max's house by now, far away from the picnicking people. Phil suddenly dragged Stevie into a private spot behind the house. "Stevie, I had to get you alone," he said, putting his arms around her. "I couldn't wait to tell you my surprise."

"What is it?" she asked. Was Phil finally going to tell her why he was in Max's office?

"I'm getting you a new bridle for your anniversary present!" Phil blurted out. "That special snaffle bridle that you wanted—it's going to be yours in a few weeks!"

Stevie stared at him. "What?" she gulped.

"I couldn't wait until our dinner tonight to tell you," Phil continued excitedly. "I know that you've been dying for one. The only thing I'm sorry about is that you couldn't use it today. But I had to order it from a catalog, so it's going to take at least two weeks . . ."

Stevie continued to stare at Phil in disbelief as he babbled on about the gift. She was shocked that he was getting her a new bridle. They were incredibly expensive! She had looked at one in a tack shop only a few weeks before, and the price was *one hundred and fifty dollars*. Phil was always complaining how broke he was. So how did he suddenly find the money to buy her a new bridle?

"That's great, Phil," she said weakly, attempting to smile. "But it's just too expensive. Besides, I didn't get you anything."

Phil didn't seem to notice Stevie's less-than-enthusiastic reaction. "I don't want a gift," he answered, giving her a little hug. "And don't worry about the cost. I can afford it now!"

Did Stevie imagine it, or did Phil put a meaningful emphasis on the word *now*? She wondered again where he had gotten all that money for the bridle. She was thrilled that she was going to finally get it, but it seemed like too much money for Phil to have or to spend.

Phil took her by the hand and they started walking again. Stevie's mind was in a whirl. *Phil . . . money . . . bridle . . .* She was starting to drive herself crazy.

Then she paused for a second and looked at her boyfriend. "What's wrong?" he asked, pulling her hair playfully. "Do I have something on my face?"

"No," Stevie said slowly. For the first time since the theft had taken place, she felt the tiniest tug of suspicion in her mind. Why did Phil have so much money all of a sudden? And why hadn't he explained his presence in Max's office yet? Why was Stevie starting to think that these two facts belonged together?

10

"So why did Phil drag you off like that? Did he have a sudden romantic urge that just couldn't wait?" teased Carole, leaning against the frame of the stable door.

The afternoon session of the rally was about to begin, and the girls had just finished getting their horses ready to go. The Saddle Club had decided to huddle briefly and figure out how to proceed with their investigation.

Stevie turned a little pink. She didn't have the heart to tell Carole and Lisa about her newfound suspicion of Phil. Besides, she consoled herself, his extravagant gift didn't *prove* anything. Maybe it just proved that she had been an extra-special girlfriend for the past six months. Maybe Phil had gotten a discount on the bridle. Didn't she know that Phil would never, ever steal anything?

"Uh, yeah," she answered, smiling brightly. "He's acting really goopy today. I think something's gotten into him, and I have to say I like it!" Carole and Lisa laughed.

To divert their attention, Stevie returned to the subject of Mo. She looked around to make sure no one was listening, then said, "Can you believe what Mo told us at lunchtime? What a bunch of losers at Mendenhall! I'm sure one of them is our thief."

Lisa agreed. "It certainly reinforces the stuff we already know about Celeste, Howard, and Kurt," she said.

"And it shows that Denise is probably not the thief," Carole said hopefully.

"Listen," Stevie said, "I've been thinking. Even if Celeste and Howard didn't steal the money, we should still try to do something about their awful behavior."

"But how?" Carole asked. "Mendenhall's pretty far away—what could we do? Besides, it's not really any of our business, and, moreover, Mo doesn't seem to want to tell anyone in authority—not Max, not the owner of Mendenhall. I don't know why. He seems like a nice guy. We've all seen him wishing the Mendenhall riders luck before they compete, and he really seems to mean it."

"Remember what Mo told us about Celeste being his favorite? If that's true, I can see how he wouldn't listen to Mo," said Lisa.

Stevie shook her head impatiently. "Well, if Mo won't speak up, why can't we? I'm not shy. Maybe it will mean more coming from outsiders, since we have nothing to gain by telling the truth about Celeste and Howard. More importantly, we have to stop Celeste and Howard from harming any more riders. If there's danger to a horse or rider involved, we should be involved, too, don't you think?"

Even Carole was forced to see the logic in that. She loved horses and riding so much, she would do anything to keep them from being harmed.

"Well, we can't solve all the problems in one day," said Lisa sensibly. "Let's just concentrate on the theft, and then later we'll figure out what to do about Celeste and Howard."

"Always the voice of reason," Stevie said, grinning at her.

"Speaking of reason," said Carole, glancing at her watch, "we've lost track of time. We're on in a few minutes, Lisa!"

"Oops," said Lisa, turning to go get Prancer. She and Carole rushed to mount up and get to the show ring.

Stevie was late on the list for the third round, so she had almost an hour to wait. Normally she would feel frustrated at having to wait so long to compete in dressage, but today was different. She had work to do!

A FEW MINUTES later, Stevie poked her head into the locker room. Almost everyone else was either competing or waiting to compete. The place was strangely silent. She had seen a rider emerge about a minute before, and then no one else came out.

"Yoo-hoo," she called tentatively. "Anyone in here?" She stepped into the room. Quickly she found Veronica's cubby and reached down and opened it. She started feeling around inside.

Stevie knew that if Max caught her snooping in Veronica's cubby, she would be in big trouble no matter what reason she came up with. But she couldn't help herself. She wanted so badly to prove that Veronica was the thief. She kept looking quickly over her shoulder, ears tuned for anyone behind her. Every noise—the creaking of the stable floor as she bent down, the far-off rustling of the few horses and ponies left in the stable— seemed especially magnified to her.

Her search, however, turned up nothing. Veronica's cubby contained exactly what Stevie should have expected: a couple of lipsticks, a hairbrush, a nail file, and an extra pair of riding gloves. Everything looked ordinary—or, rather, ordinary in Veronica terms, since her gloves looked incredibly expensive and everything else was beauty-related. But there was no money anywhere.

Then Stevie slipped out to examine Danny's stall. The gray horse wasn't there, since Veronica was in the show ring. Once again, Stevie found nothing unexpected.

Where could she be hiding the money? Stevie thought. She knew that Veronica couldn't possibly carry the money around with her. Her riding jacket and breeches were too form-fitting to hide a bulging envelope of bills. And the money from the CARL jar would weigh at least ten pounds, Stevie thought.

Taking a deep breath, Stevie decided to return to the scene of the crime—Max's office. She walked softly through the tack room, then opened the door to the office as quietly as she could and peeked in. No one was around.

She stepped in and began searching for clues. Her heart was pounding. She could feel it beating against her throat. "That's silly, you know your heart is farther down," she told herself, willing herself to calm down. She knew that if Max caught her snooping around in his office, she'd be history.

She carefully reached up and felt along the shelf where the money had been kept. Nothing. Then she examined the table under which she had found the money. Just the same old catalogs on top, and nothing on the floor but the usual dust.

Stevie sighed in frustration. Wanting to take one last look at the shelf, she stretched up on her tiptoes. Then she noticed something. A tiny scrap of something was caught on a corner of a book, near the spot where the money had been. What was it? It looked like dark fabric . . .

Stevie heard someone coming. She grabbed the scrap quickly and started to scurry out. But she was too late. Denise burst into the office and stopped short when she saw Stevie.

"Oh, hi, Stevie," she said, glancing around. She still looked pale and nervous, and her eyes darted in a jittery way.

Stevie was feeling jittery herself from her clandestine snooping. "Hi, Denise," she answered nervously.

Denise looked around the office again. She looked as if she wanted to say something but was too uncomfortable to do it.

Uh-oh, Stevie thought in despair. *She's about to ask me what I was doing in here. . . . She's going to find out I was spying. . . .* She could already see the potential scenario: Max finding out that she was a snoop and then banishing her and Belle from Pine Hollow forever.

"Uh, Stevie, can I have some privacy?" Denise asked hesitantly. "I really need to make a phone . . ."

Before Denise could finish her sentence, Stevie waved good-bye and shot out the door.

IT TOOK A good three minutes for Stevie's heart to stop thumping. While she waited it occurred to her that perhaps she wasn't cut out for a life of sneaking and snooping. Her pounding heart would set off any decent burglar alarm! Finally, feeling calmer, she took a deep breath and wandered through the indoor ring, patting some of the horses as she passed them. That was when she spotted Celeste walking ahead of her. There was something about the way she was walking and casting furtive glances around her that made Stevie highly suspicious. Celeste looked guiltier than Stevie had felt in Max's office!

Ducking behind one of the horses, Stevie waited until Celeste was gone and then checked out the indoor ring. Except for a few riders and horses, it was empty. Gold Rush and Ghost were standing tethered in a corner.

Acting on a hunch, Stevie quickly checked over Ghost. Her suspicions were soon confirmed: His right stirrup iron was dangling loosely. Someone had cut partway through the strap. It was the sort of thing no one would notice until Howard got on the horse and started to ride. The stress of riding would probably make the stirrup fall off, right in the middle of a dressage maneuver.

Stevie was furious. What a sneak Celeste was! She would even stoop to sabotage the tack of her devoted admirer!

"Celeste has *got* to be the thief," Stevie told herself. "And I'm going to prove it!" She realized, reluctantly, that she was coming to the conclusion that Veronica had nothing to do with the theft. None of the evidence pointed her way, in spite of her threats to Phil for teasing her and her blatantly ridiculous accusation.

Stevie went back to the locker room. She knew that while Veronica kept beauty supplies in her cubby, Lisa, who was a straight-A student, often kept school supplies in hers. Stevie searched through Lisa's cubby—she knew that Lisa wouldn't mind in this instance—and found a piece of paper, a pencil, and some tape. She wrote an anonymous note to Howard telling him to check his right stirrup iron before he rode Ghost again. Then she taped it to his saddle where he would be sure to see it.

Stevie hurried off to find Carole and Lisa and tell them what she had seen. On her way out of the indoor ring, she encountered Mo coming in.

"Hey!" said Mo, startled. "What's the hurry? I've been looking for you and your friends—I've got to tell you something."

"Sorry," Stevie said breathlessly. "I've got to find Carole and Lisa. I forgot to . . . uh . . . lend Carole my dressage riding whip."

"Wait, before you go," pleaded Mo, "I saw something you should know about. I'm probably all wrong—it doesn't make any sense because she's so nice and all—but that girl, Denise . . . she was in an empty stall a few minutes ago. Maybe I shouldn't say this, but . . . well, she was counting out a fistful of money!"

101

STEVIE STARED AT Mo in horror. Was it possible? Could Denise be the thief? Maybe there was some other explanation for what Mo had seen.

"Oh," Stevie said, too stunned to respond. *Denise?* "See you later." Then she abruptly left. Now she really couldn't wait to find Carole and Lisa.

She caught up with them near the show ring, standing by Prancer and Starlight. They had just finished competing in the third round of the rally, which had required a serpentine at canter, flying changes, and half-passes at trots.

"I think I was too slow on the flying change," Lisa was saying.

"No, you did great," Carole said. "I really think you'll

get a ribbon in this round." Then she saw Stevie coming up to them, and from the look on Stevie's face, she knew that the recap of the rally was temporarily stalled.

"Boy, have I got news," Stevie announced. She led them into the stable and they huddled in an empty stall, first checking to see that no one was around. Stevie quickly described what she was sure Celeste had done in the indoor ring to Howard's horse, and then, more reluctantly, she told them what Mo had said about Denise. Carole and Lisa were equally horrified.

"Mo must be mistaken," Lisa declared.

Just then Veronica walked by and caught sight of the three girls in the stall. "What is this, a meeting of the Three Stooges?"

"Not now, Veronica," Stevie said warningly. She was too upset about the recent events to get dragged into Veronica's web.

"And where's your silly boyfriend, Phil Marsten?" continued Veronica, sneering at Stevie. "I hope he decided to do the smart thing and drop out of the rally!" She walked off.

The three girls looked at each other. Veronica's tone had been unmistakably threatening. They were all thinking the same thing: Maybe they shouldn't eliminate Veronica as a suspect quite so fast. "She's really angry at Phil," said Stevie, fretting. "Maybe she's still trying to frame him!"

"I don't know," said Lisa. "I'm starting to think, from what you told us, Stevie, that Celeste is the most likely suspect. She won't stop at anything to win this rally. Why would a little thing like stealing bother her if it could destroy the competition?"

"There are just too many suspects," Stevie groaned. "Everyone's starting to look guilty!" Then she stopped for a second, remembering Phil's expensive gift to her. "Well, everyone except us and Phil," she finished. Even though she had misgivings about Phil, she didn't want Carole and Lisa to know about them yet. It was unlike Stevie to hide anything from her two best friends, but she just couldn't tell them about Phil and his sudden wealth. Somehow she felt that telling them about her suspicions might make them more . . . true.

"Let's try to figure out what Mo saw first," suggested Carole. "Maybe we can just talk to Denise and tell her what's going on."

Lisa looked thoughtful. "Denise is an incredibly honest person," she said slowly. "If we confront her about what Mo saw, and we're not mean about it, maybe we can convince her to confess and give the money back."

"And Max really likes Denise, so maybe he'll forgive her," added Stevie.

The three girls searched the stable. Then Stevie remembered that she had last seen Denise in Max's office.

They went there immediately. The door to the office was still closed, and they could hear Denise talking on the phone. By pressing their ears to the door, the girls could just make out what she was saying. Even though they felt guilty about eavesdropping, they were too curious to leave. Besides, maybe Denise would provide the answer herself and save them from accusing her.

"Really?" Denise was saying excitedly. "That's wonderful!"

Carole raised her eyebrows questioningly at Lisa and Stevie. They shrugged in response, equally puzzled.

"Expenses plus tuition! That's fabulous! Thank you so much! Yes, I'll fill out the paperwork as soon as I get it! Thank you, thank you!"

A second later, Denise flung open the door and Stevie almost fell into the office, she had been listening so hard. But Denise didn't seem the least bit surprised to see the three girls hanging on the door frame. She broke into an enormous grin. "Carole, Lisa, Stevie!" she exclaimed. "I've got wonderful news!"

"What is it?" asked Carole.

"I just got a full scholarship for the rest of my college education!" said Denise, laughing joyfully. "Full tuition, plus room and board. I applied to a foundation run by a woman who's crazy about horses, and they called me today!"

The Saddle Club cheered in delight and gave Denise a big four-way hug, after which Denise collapsed wearily into Max's chair.

"I've been making myself sick with worry," she told the girls. "I've been so anxious lately because I couldn't figure out how I could stay in college. I thought I'd have to quit and go back to Indiana to find a job."

Suddenly Denise slapped herself on the forehead. "What am I thinking?" she blurted out. "I've got to tell Red. He's been worried, too. I was crying on his shoulder just this morning. See you later, girls—and good luck in the rally!" She hurried out of the office.

The three girls walked out of the office a second later. "Do you know what this means?" Carole asked happily.

Lisa nodded. "It means that Denise is innocent! I'm so glad. And I'm gladder still that her money problems are over."

"But then what did Mo see?" Stevie wondered out loud.

"She must have been mistaken," Carole said reassuringly. "Denise was probably counting her own money and worrying about her budget. And then Mo exaggerated, in her own head, how much money Denise really had in her hand. You know how it is. She's probably got money on the brain, because everyone's thinking too much about the theft. I know I am," she finished with a grimace.

"We're no closer to finding the thief," said Stevie, frustrated.

"Yes, we are," Lisa reminded her softly. "We know now that it's not Denise."

Stevie grinned, acknowledging Lisa's point. "You're right. That matters a lot. Well, who's left?" she asked determinedly.

Carole and Lisa exchanged glances. They knew why Stevie was so focused on finding the thief. After Veronica's very public accusation of Phil, Stevie was desperate to clear his name once and for all. And although they didn't know it, Stevie was starting to get really worried. She was thinking about Phil's very expensive gift, and that little niggle of suspicion surfaced again.

She pushed the thought away firmly. "So now we're down to Veronica, Celeste, Howard, and Kurt," she said. "And, technically, Mo, although we've basically crossed her off, too."

Suddenly Stevie remembered the scrap she had found in Max's office. "Look, I think I found a clue in Max's office, on the shelf where the money was." She dug it out of her jacket pocket, and Carole and Lisa bent over her hand for a closer look. It was a piece of black yarn, the type that they all used to braid their horses' manes.

"What does that tell us?" Carole asked.

"Nothing, that's what," said Stevie, discouraged.

"Practically everyone here is walking around with bits of black yarn clinging to them!" She stuck it back into her pocket and checked her watch. She gasped. "I'm going to be late for my turn!" She hastily ran off to compete in the third round of the rally.

12

CAROLE WAITED FOR her turn in the fourth and final round of the dressage rally. She was already mounted, since she was scheduled to go next.

The fourth round of the rally was the most difficult and challenging series of tests, stopping just short of international-level dressage tests. Most of the junior riders didn't even enter that round, instead competing only for individual ribbons in the first three rounds. But only riders who competed in all the rounds could hope to place for an overall ribbon, which was based on point totals from all four rounds.

The fourth round involved standard dressage movements like flying changes and pirouettes. Asking a horse to execute quick steps while cantering required a lot of training and practice. Carole could feel her concentration becoming more intense, and she could tell that Starlight was getting eager, too.

Mo was performing, and Carole watched as she and Indy executed a perfect pirouette. "He really does look like Starlight," Carole murmured to herself. She began examining Indy from stem to stern, noting all the differences. Indy's ears were slightly larger. His star was a slightly different shape. He was a tiny bit heavier than Starlight. And something about his black tail looked different, too. Was it its arch?

Carole kept turning the question over and over again in her head until she realized that she was in danger of losing her concentration for her upcoming turn. "Why am I obsessing about this now?" she asked herself, annoyed. "Who cares if their tails are different?" She looked again at Indy's black tail, which was braided, like Starlight's, along the length of his dock.

Then she gasped. She had just realized what was bothering her, and it was something that could break their case wide open! Frantically she looked around for Lisa and Stevie.

"The next rider is Carole Hanson, representing Horse Wise," Max announced. Carole was startled. She took a deep breath and managed to collect herself. The mystery would have to wait a few more minutes.

* * *

LISA HAD ALREADY finished her final turn in the rally. She was in Prancer's stall, removing the mare's tack. She had filled the water bucket and promised to give the tired horse a complete grooming later on, after the rally.

The minute Lisa removed Prancer's bridle, the mare again turned her head and nipped at Lisa's sleeve. Then she butted Lisa hard with her nose.

"What is wrong with you?" asked Lisa, exasperated. She always tried to be patient with Prancer—or with any horse—but she was starting to reach the end of her rope with the horse's strange behavior. What on earth could be wrong with her?

THE ORDER OF competition changed for each round of the rally, and Stevie had been early on the list for the fourth round. She and Belle had done really well, although Stevie felt that that was more because of Belle than her. In a corner of her mind, she was gratified to realize that all the practice and training she and Belle had put into dressage was paying off. After finishing her turn, she stabled Belle and turned her full attention to the investigation again. She wandered around the stable thinking so hard that she almost bumped into spectators several times.

Who was the thief? Was it Celeste? Everything Stevie

had learned about Celeste was definitely bad—her competitiveness, her total power over Howard.

Was it Kurt? Stevie couldn't dismiss what Mo had told them about Kurt's past, and she was definitely puzzled by Kurt's general weirdness.

Could it be . . . ? Stevie tried to push the thought of Phil from her mind. But why was Phil lying about being in Max's office? Phil couldn't be the thief. She knew him too well, and she knew that he could never steal money.

Then Stevie stopped short. "But where did he get the money to pay for my gift?" she asked herself. She clutched her head distractedly. All these questions, and not a single answer.

I'll go back to Max's office, she decided. Maybe more clues would turn up, or at least a better clue than a stupid piece of yarn.

She walked into the tack room and stopped. She hated going back into Max's office. Her spying in there had nearly given her a nervous breakdown last time. She sat down on a trunk to calm herself. On the one hand, she reasoned, she really needed more clues. On the other hand, Denise had caught her in there once, and Stevie was still thankful that Denise had been so preoccupied with her own affairs that she hadn't questioned Stevie's presence there.

As Stevie silently argued with herself, Kurt walked

into the tack room. He didn't notice Stevie sitting in the corner, and he put his hand on the doorknob to Max's office. Then he paused. He looked nervous, and Stevie distinctly saw him gulp as if he was gathering his courage to go in.

Stevie's eyes widened. Kurt looked really nervous. What was he about to do? Why did he look so strange? Then her jaw dropped. Maybe Kurt was returning to the scene of the crime! She jumped up and confronted him. "I knew it!" she said triumphantly, forgetting all of her suspicions about Veronica, Celeste, Howard, and Phil. "You're the thief. You took the money, and you're coming back for more!"

Kurt was badly shaken by Stevie's sudden appearance. He turned as white as a sheet and collapsed against the door to Max's office. Then he saw who it was and his expression turned surly again. "You nearly scared me half to death," he snarled.

"Oh, don't change the subject," Stevie said menacingly. "I know now who stole the money. You're guilty. Where did you hide it? Give it back right away."

Kurt looked bewildered. "Listen," he said firmly. "I don't know what you're talking about, and I barely know who you are, other than your name. Nor do I care. But will you please go away? I was right in the middle of something."

"Yeah, I know what you were in the middle of," Stevie

said. "You were going back to steal more money from Max's office!"

Kurt put his hands in the air in frustration. "What money? Why do you keep talking about money?" he asked.

"Don't play innocent with me," Stevie sneered. "You were there with the rest of us. You saw how much money Max hid on that shelf."

"Yeah, and so?" Kurt asked.

"And so you took it," Stevie said. Then she stopped and looked at him. Kurt was a picture of puzzlement. He was gazing blankly at her as if she were speaking Greek. Now *she* was getting confused. Unless Kurt was a really good actor—and so far, she had only seen him act one part, that of the rude loner—he was telling the truth about not understanding her.

Once Stevie began pursuing an idea, it was hard for her to slow down. But she also had a strong sense of fair play. And besides, she and Kurt were getting nowhere in this conversation. She took a deep breath and decided to soften her interrogation. "Listen, Kurt," she said patiently. "All that money we saw in Max's office was stolen not long after we were in there. I've been trying to find out ever since then who took the money, especially since everyone at the rally probably thinks my boyfriend, Phil, did it."

Despite his habitual reticence, Kurt was beginning to

114

look interested. "Why would everyone think that?" he asked.

"Because Veronica—the rotten egg at Pine Hollow—accused him in front of everyone," said Stevie. "Weren't you there when Max announced the theft?"

Kurt shook his head. "No, I had no idea. I've been hanging out by myself ever since I got to this stable."

Stevie had no trouble believing that. It pretty much fit in with what little she knew about Kurt. And somehow, she was starting to get a feeling that maybe she was wrong about Kurt being the thief. After all, they were now talking almost like normal, friendly people. Kurt was not exactly Mr. Congeniality, but at least he was standing there, not running away, and giving what appeared to be honest answers to Stevie's accusations.

She needed to clear up one last question, though. "What were you doing, going into Max's office all by yourself?" she asked.

She almost wished she hadn't asked the question, because Kurt's expression became sullen again. "That's none of your business," he said, turning away.

Stevie grabbed his arm impulsively. "Please tell me," she said. "I know you can't be crazy about someone who calls you a thief, but I've got to know. I've got to find out who did this so I can eliminate Phil as a suspect."

"You wouldn't understand," Kurt muttered. "You and your horse-crazy friends just wouldn't get it."

Stevie put her hands on her hips. "Try me," she said decisively. "I might surprise you."

Kurt gave a heavy sigh. "I was just going to use Max's phone."

"Why?" Stevie asked.

Kurt sighed again. "I needed to call my parents."

"Why?" Stevie asked again. "What could be so urgent?" She knew she was being relentless, but getting information out of Kurt was like pulling teeth.

"Because I hate riding, that's why!" Kurt blurted out. "I hate riding, and I'm terrified of horses. I can't even stand to be around my own horse, Simon, even though I know he's one of the nicest horses in the world." He stopped and took a deep breath.

"You hate riding?" Stevie asked. Now she was more confused than ever. What did this have to do with anything?

"Yeah," said Kurt. Now that he had said it out loud, he appeared almost relieved. "My whole family is really into horses. My dad's a well-known horse trainer. My parents couldn't believe it when I was scared of horses. I didn't want to have anything to do with them. I'm more interested in physics and astronomy and working for NASA someday.

"But my parents refused to understand," he continued. "So they forced me to join Mendenhall, and they bought me Simon. Do you know what it's like," he added in a plaintive tone, "to be surrounded by horse-crazy people? Do you know what it's like when your parents eat, breathe, and sleep horses and can't understand why you don't feel the same way? And do you know what it's like when the only people you meet are like you, people who are as horse-crazy as my family? I knew you guys would think I was a freak once you found out how I really felt. That's why I acted like a jerk—what's the point of even trying?"

"But what does this have to do with your being in Max's office?" Stevie asked.

"I got up the courage to talk to Max today," Kurt said. "The owner of Mendenhall won't listen to me—my parents board ten horses at his stable. Worse yet, he's best friends with them. He's ridden with them ever since they were all little kids. He also can't believe that I'm not into horses. But Max understood. He told me to come in here and call my parents and to be firm with them about quitting riding. He even offered to talk to them if I wanted. But I don't think I'll need him. I've made up my mind." He straightened his shoulders and stuck out his chin determinedly.

"You're not the thief," said Stevie in wonder.

"No, I'm not," answered Kurt.

Now Stevie believed him. She stuck out her hand. "I'm sorry I suspected you," she said. After a moment's hesitation, Kurt took her hand and shook it. "And I don't think you should jump to conclusions about everyone. You're right, my friends and I are crazy about horses. And I can understand how we would appear to you; we must seem just like your family. But we like other things, too." Stevie searched her brain to think of other hobbies the girls had in common. At the moment she couldn't think of any—a dilemma Carole and Lisa would have found hilarious. "Anyway, we're always willing to listen to other people's problems," she said instead. "I think it's great that you're going to do your own thing."

Kurt looked at her for a long moment. "Thanks," he said finally. "I think I believe you. And I'm sorry for being so rude to you and your friends. Now if you don't mind, I'd like some privacy." He went into Max's office.

As Stevie walked out of the tack room, she mulled over Kurt's story in her mind. She found it interesting— and incomprehensible, too, since she couldn't understand how someone could be afraid of horses. *I guess it would be like me having to join . . . the math club, or something like that, and go to meetings every day of the week*, she thought.

Suddenly she realized something. Kurt's explanation meant that a huge problem still remained. The theft was still unsolved because now his strange behavior was completely explained. Not only that, but they still had four suspects left! She winced as she remembered Phil's strange behavior and his unexplained wealth. Maybe they had *five* suspects left!

Stevie went to find Carole and Lisa. She bumped into them in the stable aisle as they were looking for her.

Carole grabbed her by the arm. "We were just looking for you."

Stevie nodded. "I have some news for you, too. Emergency Saddle Club meeting—right now!"

The three girls went into the tack room, which was still empty. Carole started talking in a rush. "I have a new theory about how to solve the crime! I know a way to eliminate almost all of our suspects!"

"Wait!" Stevie interrupted her, in her usual impulsive fashion. "I can *definitely* eliminate at least one of the subjects." She told them what Kurt had said.

"Poor Kurt," said Lisa when Stevie was finished. "Imagine being forced to do something you hate—although I can't imagine being scared of horses."

Carole had listened to Stevie in silence. As Stevie's story sank in, she looked up, her eyes shining. "So Kurt is out as a suspect," she said slowly.

"I couldn't doubt his story," said Stevie. "I couldn't believe," she added, giggling, "how totally *sincere* someone could be about hating horses!"

"Then I know exactly who the thief is," Carole said excitedly. She leaned forward and began telling Lisa and Stevie her theory.

* * *

A FEW MINUTES later, the three girls emerged from the tack room. They quickly searched the stable and then the indoor ring.

Mo was standing in the ring, feeding Indy an apple. When The Saddle Club saw her, they walked up to her and said hello.

"Hey," Stevie said eagerly. "We need your help, Mo. We know who stole the money, and we want to set a trap for the thief!"

Mo's eyes sparkled. "What great news!" she said. "I'll do anything to help."

Carole grabbed her arm and began pulling her toward the stable. "Come this way," she said.

"The trap is in the tack room," Lisa whispered to Mo.

Mo allowed herself to be dragged to the tack room. Along the way, she excitedly asked questions.

"Celeste and Howard did it, didn't they? They're always up to something," Mo said.

"You'll see," Carole replied enigmatically.

Mo stopped suddenly, a look of horror on her face. "Oh, no, it's not your friend Denise, is it?" she asked. "She's so nice. But then again, I did see her counting all that money."

"It's not Denise," Stevie said. She pulled Mo's sleeve to get her moving again. The four girls entered the stable and walked toward the tack room.

"Well, that's a relief," said Mo. "I really like her. I

guess Veronica really had it in for your boyfriend, right? She took the money to get her revenge, huh?"

Stevie shrugged. "Veronica always has it in for one of us," she said cheerfully. "But money is one thing she doesn't need."

"C'mon, you guys," Mo said impatiently. "Who did it? How are we going to trap the thief?"

"Shhh," whispered Carole. She looked around nervously. "Mustn't talk here. Not safe."

"Yes, we have to make sure the trap works perfectly and the thief suspects nothing," added Stevie.

When they entered the tack room, the group first made sure that no one else was there. Then Stevie carefully shut the door behind her. She swung around to face Mo. "The trap has worked," she said. "We know everything, Mo. *You* took the money!"

Mo gasped. "Wh-Wh-What are you talking about?" she stammered, turning pale underneath her freckles. "How could you say such a thing?"

Carole stepped forward. She had a stern expression on her face. "We've all been doing a little investigating," she said. "We knew we needed to clear Phil's name and to get that money back to Max. We realized that the thief had to be someone who saw Max hide the money on that shelf."

"And then we eliminated suspects, one by one," said Lisa.

"We knew it couldn't be one of us," said Stevie. "And we knew it couldn't be Phil, either."

"Then we found out more about Denise and Kurt," said Lisa.

"Then I figured it out," Carole said proudly. "Stevie found a bit of black yarn on the shelf. The thief was someone who needed black yarn for their horse's mane. That eliminated Celeste, Howard, and Veronica as suspects. None of their horses have black manes! Gold Rush is a palomino, and Ghost and Danny are both gray. Only you and Kurt have bay horses with black manes and tails, and we've just ruled out Kurt. That leaves you, Mo. You're the thief!"

Mo looked as if she were about to protest her innocence again, but then her expression became sly and cunning. Suddenly she no longer seemed like the friendly girl they had met just several hours before. If they had had any doubt about her guilt, her expression now confirmed it. "What about your boyfriend, Phil?" she asked Stevie. "He rides a bay gelding, too. Your little theory doesn't prove anything."

"Phil would never steal money," replied Stevie. "He's known Max for too long, and we know Phil too well. Give it up, Mo. We know you did it."

Mo's face crumpled, and her eyes filled with tears. She began sobbing. "I needed that money!" she wailed. "You

122

don't understand! My family doesn't understand me. I have no friends."

"What does that have to do with anything?" Lisa asked.

"I decided to run away from home last night," Mo said. "I knew I could get a head start if I left from here, since it's so far from home. But I needed money. When I saw how much was in the envelope and the jar, I didn't stop to think. I just took it!"

Carole, Lisa, and Stevie were disconcerted. Mo sounded so desperate. What was going on in her life? How badly did she need that money?

"Maybe running away isn't the answer," Lisa said.

"What do you know?" Mo asked. Her tone was so bitter that Stevie felt a pang. She knew by looking at Carole and Lisa that the initial anger and triumph behind their accusations were fading and that they were all starting to worry about what could be so terribly wrong with Mo's life.

Just then the door from Max's office opened and Kurt walked in. Mo took advantage of the open door to scurry away before they could stop her. She was in such a hurry that she collided with Kurt, nearly knocking him over. "Hey, where's the fire?" he said, irritated.

"Let her go," Stevie said. "We should tell Max what happened and let him handle it." She then looked at

Kurt, who, to her complete shock, was grinning happily. They had all gotten used to Kurt's dour expression. He looked weird with a big smile plastered on his face.

"Hey, good news," he announced. "I did it! I convinced my parents to let me quit riding!"

The girls were silent for a second; then Carole spoke. "Uh, congratulations?" she said in a doubtful tone. Stevie added her own lukewarm support.

Lisa smiled at Kurt. "We're really happy for you," she explained. "We're just having a little trouble understanding how someone could hate riding. But now you can do what you want, and that's terrific."

Gruffly Kurt said, "Well, listen, I've already explained myself to Stevie, so I'm not going to go through it again. I'm sorry I was such a jerk to you this morning. I really didn't know how I was going to go through with the rally. But Max helped me out, and I feel loads better." The girls could tell that he was uncomfortable talking about it, so they didn't press for details. Kurt jerked a thumb in the direction in which Mo had vanished. "What's wrong with Mo? Is she acting up again?"

The girls exchanged glances. "What do you mean, *again?*" asked Stevie.

"She's a real problem at Mendenhall," Kurt replied. "She's always lying, teasing other people, and generally causing serious trouble. She's been kicked out of too many riding lessons to count."

Although Carole, Lisa, and Stevie had witnessed for themselves how devious Mo could be, they were still shocked at Kurt's news. "So Celeste didn't arrange for Howard to injure her main rival and put her in the hospital for weeks?" Stevie asked.

"What?" asked Kurt, startled. The Saddle Club filled him in on the story Mo had told them.

"Well, Celeste *is* kind of ruthless," chuckled Kurt. "And she *does* treat Howard like her personal servant. But she pretty much keeps to herself. That thing with Mo's tack was really payback for something Mo did to her last week. When Celeste was practicing, Mo blew up a brown paper bag and popped it. Gold Rush almost bolted and threw Celeste, but she's such a good rider, she managed to calm him down."

The three girls looked at each other. Mo's story about Celeste and Howard was true—only Mo was the culprit and Celeste was the victim!

Then they told Kurt how they had discovered that Mo was the thief. "We were totally taken in by her," Carole said ruefully.

"Yeah," said Stevie. "She even told us that you and your two brothers were in trouble with the law and that you had to report to a probation officer once a week."

Kurt looked insulted. "I don't have any brothers and I've never even gotten detention at school," he said.

Stevie shook her head. "Wow," she said. "That was some snow job she did on us."

Lisa agreed. "And to think we wanted her to join Pine Hollow! She made us think she wanted to switch stables so badly because of Celeste."

"Not to mention the fact that she tried to incriminate Denise," put in Carole. "How mean can someone get?"

"Pretty mean," said Stevie. "I bet that *she* was the one who sabotaged Howard's stirrup. I just assumed that Celeste had done it because we knew how determined she was to win the rally and because I saw her coming out of the indoor ring around that time. But Mo was in there, too."

Kurt nodded. "It was definitely Mo. She's pulled that stunt on a couple of riders at Mendenhall. And the only reason she wants to switch stables so badly is that the owner is finally at the end of his patience. He's kept her on for so long because Mo's parents have begged him to, and because Mo takes really good care of Indy. But lately she's started to put a lot of riders and horses in danger."

Lisa suddenly remembered what Mo had told them about her problems. "Maybe she had a good reason for taking that money," she said. "She told us how desperate she was to run away. Maybe things are really bad at home

126

for her right now and she's acting out her frustration at the stable."

Kurt shook his head. "That doesn't explain everything," he said. "My parents know Mo's parents. They're in the process of getting a divorce, and I know Mo is taking it hard. But they're also two really nice people. They're trying to make things as fair as possible for Mo, and the two of them have been spending tons of time with her. I don't know everything," he added, "but I know that whatever is going on with Mo's life, it's not enough to make her act the way she's been acting. She's put a lot of us at Mendenhall in real danger, and now this."

"I have a hunch that the owner of Mendenhall is about to get a really good reason to bar Mo from that stable—permanently," Stevie said grimly.

After saying good-bye to Kurt, the three girls hurried off to find Max and tell him they had solved the mystery.

13

"I'M SO TIRED," groaned Stevie, leaning against her broom.
She had just finished sweeping the tack room floor.

"Amen," agreed Carole, who was polishing tack. "But
you can't be tired, Stevie. You've got an anniversary dinner ahead of you."

Stevie flopped down on a bench. For the last hour,
ever since the rally had ended, the two girls had been
working hard to clean up the stable and take care of their
horses. "I've had all the excitement I can take," she said.
"I thought the rally was going to be the main event today. Then comes the dinner. Then the theft. Then the
investigation. I need a break!"

"Don't forget about winning the blue ribbon in the
second round and placing second overall in the dressage

128

rally," Carole reminded Stevie. "That was pretty amazing, especially after everything that happened today."

"You guys didn't do so badly, either," replied Stevie, grinning. Carole had won a blue ribbon for the first round and had placed third in the overall competition. Lisa had won a red ribbon in the third round and had placed sixth for the overall rally.

"So Celeste ended up winning the whole competition after all," mused Carole.

"She really is a terrific rider," Stevie said grudgingly. "But just wait until next time! If the next rally is crime-free, she doesn't stand a chance against us!"

Carole laughed. They finished cleaning and organizing the tack room and went to find Lisa.

Lisa was in Prancer's stall, finishing her grooming. "Hey," she said when she saw them. "I still can't figure out what's wrong with this horse. She keeps nipping me and she won't stand still. It's taken three times as long as usual to groom her."

"I forgot about Prancer," said Stevie. "With everything that's happened today, Prancer's weirdness just slipped my mind."

"I know what you mean," said Lisa. "I was just thinking how I really liked Mo at first. I still can't believe that she could be so sneaky. Telling us all those lies, and we believed her!"

"We all liked her," Carole said. "Maybe we liked her

because we thought Celeste, Howard, and Kurt were so awful at first. And maybe I liked her because Starlight and Indy look so much alike. And actually, Celeste and Howard really didn't improve, even after we found out about Mo!"

"What happened to Mo after we told Max?" asked Lisa.

Stevie looked grim. "I just ran into Max," she told them. "Mo *did* get kicked out of Mendenhall. Her parents were at the rally today, and they're really upset by this latest incident. They've already got Mo going to therapy, but now they're enrolling her in a program that deals with troubled kids. The program lasts three months. Apparently they can visit her once a week, but otherwise Mo's going to go through an intensive period of counseling and activities. The program is run on a farm, and Mo can ride horses and help take care of the animals there. Horses, and animals in general, seem to be the only thing that works for her."

"I'm glad Max agreed not to press charges," Lisa said softly. "Even if Mo is a troublemaker, clearly she needs a lot of help."

Just then Phil stuck his head into the stall. The girls noticed that he was carrying the picnic hamper. "Are you talking about me again?" he said, grinning. "I just can't seem to help being the center of attention!"

"Oh, please," answered Stevie, smiling fondly at him. "Get over yourself, will you?"

Phil pretended to look wounded. "I was just coming to tell you," he told Stevie, "that it's starting to drizzle outside."

"So much for our beautiful day! I can't believe it's raining again," complained Stevie.

"Don't worry, I've rearranged everything," Phil said. "I've cleared a nice, cozy spot for our picnic in the hayloft. You can join me there at your leisure."

"We were just talking about the theft," Carole informed him. "You interrupted a very important discussion."

Phil groaned. "I am so sick of talking about today," he complained. "So what if Mo is a thief? Her crime was amateur, a totally clumsy job."

"Oh, and you're the expert?" Stevie asked sarcastically, forgetting that, for a while, that had actually been her main worry.

"Well, I've pulled off a couple of schemes in my time," Phil boasted. "Nothing criminal, though. As a matter of fact, I managed to hatch a little plot this week. I made up that whole story about saving money so that I could buy Teddy some extra-special feed. I was really saving up for a fancy dinner tonight. And you never suspected a thing!"

Stevie was touched. "Really?" she asked excitedly. "Are we going out tonight?"

"But then you kept dreaming about that bridle," Phil continued proudly. "So I checked the price of it in one of the catalogs from Max's office. Then I caught up with your parents at lunchtime and they agreed to chip in half the cost. They said to tell you it's an early Christmas gift for you."

Stevie threw her arms around Phil and gave him a big hug. "That's why you were in Max's office—to look at catalogs!" she said happily.

Phil grinned. "Yeah, and that's why I couldn't tell you the reason. Hey," he said suddenly with a worried frown, "you didn't think I was guilty of stealing that money, did you?"

Stevie gazed at him adoringly. "Not for a second," she told him. She knew that a little fib, under these circumstances, was okay.

"But here's the bad news," said Phil. "Now that I'm getting you the bridle, I can't buy you dinner tonight. So it really is a picnic in the hayloft—with sandwiches and potato chips. Nothing glamorous."

"I think those sandwiches will taste like the finest French cuisine to Stevie right about now," Carole joked, looking at Stevie's face.

Stevie's eyes were shining. She was thinking about how hard Phil had worked to surprise her. She also

132

couldn't help thinking about the new bridle she was getting in a few weeks! She and Phil said good-bye to Carole and Lisa and climbed up the ladder to the hayloft.

The hayloft smelled dusty-sweet. Phil had cleared a large space and spread out a blanket for their picnic. "I brought candles, but I don't think we should light them here," he said. "We might set the hay on fire."

"It doesn't matter one bit," Stevie assured him. As they sat down and began unpacking the picnic basket, they heard a loud scurrying sound.

Stevie jumped to her feet. "What was that?" she asked, startled.

"Look!" Phil pointed. "Remember what Doc Tock said last week about animals in the area?"

Stevie looked in the corner and saw a large raccoon. Behind it were four baby raccoons, staring at Stevie and Phil with round, frightened eyes.

"Doc Tock said that raccoons were always getting into people places," said Phil. "She didn't mention them getting into *horse* places."

The raccoons were so cute that Stevie melted. "They're adorable," she said. Suddenly the raccoons jumped, then disappeared through a hole in the corner of the loft.

"Hey!" Stevie exclaimed. She scrambled over to look at the hole through which the raccoon family had vanished. A thought struck her. "Phil, I'll be right back," she told him, and climbed down the ladder.

Carole and Lisa were still in Prancer's stall. "I think I've solved another mystery," Stevie told them. "I think I know why Prancer has been acting so strange." But Carole and Lisa were absorbed with calming down an agitated Prancer.

"Shhh," Lisa said soothingly, patting the mare's nose. Carole was gently rubbing Prancer's neck.

"A band of raccoons just ran through here," Lisa explained to Stevie. "Prancer was terrified of them. I guess that in addition to cats, she doesn't like raccoons, either."

"Especially when they're stealing her food," Stevie said triumphantly. "Those raccoons live in the hayloft right above Prancer's stall. Remember how Doc Tock said that raccoons will rummage through people's garbage cans? I bet those raccoons have been eating Prancer's feed!"

Lisa gaped at Stevie. "So all this time Prancer has been *hungry?*" she asked in astonishment. Suddenly Prancer's odd behavior—her constant nibbling and head-butting—began to make sense.

"What other explanation is there?" asked Stevie.

Lisa grinned happily and turned to give Prancer a hug. "You poor thing," she said. "I'm going to get you some more feed right away."

134

"And I'm going to ask Max to call CARL to come and get this raccoon family relocated to a new home," said Carole, heading toward Max's office.

"Well, I know what I've got to do," said Stevie, looking meaningfully toward the hayloft. "I've got a six-month anniversary to celebrate!"

What happens to The Saddle Club next?
Read Bonnie Bryant's exciting new series
and find out.

High school. Driver's licenses. Boyfriends. Jobs.

A lot of new things are happening, but one thing remains the same: Stevie Lake, Lisa Atwood, and Carole Hanson are still best friends. However, even among best friends some things do change, and problems can strain any friendship . . . but these three can handle it. Can't they?

Read an excerpt from Pine Hollow #1: *The Long Ride*.

PROLOGUE

"Do you think we'll get there in time?" Stevie Lake asked, looking around for some reassuring sign that the airport was near.

"Since that plane almost landed on us, I think it's safe to say that we're close," Carole Hanson said.

"Turn right here," said Callie Forester from the backseat.

"And then left up ahead," Carole advised, picking out directions from the signs that flashed past near the airport entrance. "I think Lisa's plane is leaving from that terminal there."

"Which one?"

"The one we just passed," Callie said.

"Oh," said Stevie. She gripped the steering wheel tightly and looked for a way to turn around without causing a major traffic tie-up.

"This would be easier if we were on horseback," said Carole.

"Everything's easier on horseback," Stevie agreed.

"Or if we had a police escort," said Callie.

"Have you done that?" Stevie asked, trying to maneuver the car across three lanes of traffic.

"I have," said Callie. "It's kind of fun, but dangerous. It makes you think you're almost as important as other people tell you you are."

Stevie rolled her window down and waved wildly at the confused drivers around her. Clearly, her waving confused them more, but it worked. All traffic stopped. She crossed the necessary three lanes and pulled onto the service road.

It took another ten minutes to get back to the right and then ten more to find a parking place. Five minutes into the terminal. And then all that was left was to find Lisa.

"Where do you think she is?" Carole asked.

"I know," said Stevie. "Follow me."

"That's what we've been doing all morning," Callie said dryly. "And look how far it's gotten us."

But she followed anyway.

ALEX LAKE REACHED across the table in the airport cafeteria and took Lisa Atwood's hand.

"It's going to be a long summer," he said.

Lisa nodded. Saying good-bye was one of her least favorite activities. She didn't want Alex to know how hard it was, though. That would just make it tougher on him. The two of them had known each other for four years—as long as Lisa had been best friends with Alex's twin sister, Stevie. But they'd only started dating six months earlier. Lisa could hardly believe that. It seemed as if she'd been in love with him forever.

"But it is just for the summer," she said. The words sounded dumb even as they came out of her mouth. The summer *was* long. She wouldn't come back to Virginia until right before school started.

"I wish your dad didn't live so far away, and I wish the summer weren't so long."

"It'll go fast," said Lisa.

"For you, maybe. You'll be in California, surfing or something. I'll just be here, mowing lawns."

"I've never surfed in my life—"

"Until now," said Alex. It was almost a challenge, and Lisa didn't like it.

"I don't want to fight with you," said Lisa.

"I don't want to fight with you, either," he said, relenting. "I'm sorry. It's just that I want things to be different. Not very different. Just a little different."

"Me too," said Lisa. She squeezed his hand. It was a way to keep from saying anything else, because she was afraid that if she tried to speak she might cry, and she hated it when she cried. It made her face red and puffy, but most of all, it told other people how she was feeling. She'd found it useful to keep her feelings to herself these days. Like Alex, she wanted things to be different, but she wanted them to be very different, not just a little. She sighed. That was slightly better than crying.

"I TOLD YOU SO," said Stevie to Callie and Carole.

Stevie had threaded her way through the airport terminal, straight to the cafeteria near the security checkpoint. And there, sitting next to the door, were her twin brother and her best friend.

"Surprise!" the three girls cried, crowding around the table.

"We just couldn't let you be the only one to say good-bye to Lisa," Carole said, sliding into the booth next to Alex.

"We had to be here, too. You understand that, don't you?" Stevie asked Lisa as she sat down next to her.

"And since I was in the car, they brought me along," said Callie, pulling up a chair from a nearby table.

"You guys!" said Lisa, her face lighting up with joy. "I'm so glad you're here. I was afraid I wasn't going to see you for months and months!"

She *was* glad they were there. It wouldn't have felt right if she'd had to leave without seeing them one more time. "I thought you had other things to do."

"We just told you that so we could surprise you. We did surprise you, didn't we?"

"You surprised me," Lisa said, beaming.

"Me too," Alex said dryly. "I'm surprised, too. I really thought I could go for an afternoon, just *one* afternoon of my life, without seeing my twin sister."

Stevie grinned. "Well, there's always tomorrow," she said. "And that's something to look forward to, right?"

"Right," he said, grinning back.

Since she was closest to the outside, Callie went and got sodas for herself, Stevie, and Carole. When she rejoined the group, they were talking about everything in the world except the fact that Lisa was going to be gone for the summer and how much they were all going to miss one another.

She passed the drinks around and sat quietly at the end of the table. There wasn't much for her to say. She didn't really feel as if she belonged there. She wasn't anybody's best friend. It wasn't as if they minded her being there, but she'd come along because Stevie had offered to drive her to a tack shop after they left the airport. She was simply along for the ride.

". . . And don't forget to say hello to Skye."

"Skye? Skye who?" asked Alex.

"Don't pay any attention to him," Lisa said. "He's just jealous."

"You mean because Skye is a movie star?"

"And say hi to your father and the new baby. It must be exciting that you'll meet your sister."

"Well, of course, you've already met her, but now she's crawling, right? It's a whole different thing."

An announcement over the PA system brought their chatter to a sudden halt.

"It's my flight," Lisa said slowly. "They're starting to board and I've got to get through security and then to Gate . . . whatever."

"Fourteen," Alex said. "It comes after Gate Twelve. There are no thirteens in airports."

"Let's go."

"Here, I'll carry that."

"And I'll get this one . . ."

As Callie watched, Lisa hugged Carole and Stevie. Then she kissed Alex. Then she hugged her friends again. Then she turned to Alex.

"I think it's time for us to go," Carole said tactfully.

"Write or call every day," Stevie said.

"It's a promise," said Lisa. "Thanks for coming to the airport. You, too, Callie."

Callie smiled and gave Lisa a quick hug before all the girls backed off from Lisa and Alex.

Lisa waved. Her friends waved and turned to leave her alone with Alex. They were all going to miss her, but the girls had one another. Alex only had his lawns to mow. He needed the last minutes with Lisa.

"See you at home!" Stevie called over her shoulder, but she didn't think Alex heard. His attention was completely focused on one person.

Carole wiped a tear from her eye once they'd rounded a corner. "I'm going to miss her."

"Me too," said Stevie.

Carole turned to Callie. "It must be hard for you to understand," she said.

"Not really," said Callie. "I can tell you three are really close."

"We are," Carole said. "Best friends for a long time. We're practically inseparable." Even to her the words sounded exclusive and uninviting. If Callie noticed, she didn't say anything.

The three girls walked out of the terminal and found their way to Stevie's car. As she turned on the engine, Stevie was aware of an uncomfortable empty feeling. She really didn't like the idea of Lisa's being gone for the summer, and her own unhappiness was not going to be helped by a brother who was going to spend the entire time moping about his missing girlfriend. There had to be something that would make her feel better.

"Say, Carole, do you want to come along with us to the tack shop?" she asked.

"No, I can't," Carole said. "I promised I'd bring in the horses from the paddock before dark, so you can just drop me off at Pine Hollow. Anyway, aren't you due at work in an hour?"

Stevie glanced at her watch. Carole was right. Everything was taking longer than it was supposed to this afternoon.

"Don't worry," Callie said quickly. "We can go to the tack shop another time."

"You don't mind?" Stevie asked.

"No. I don't. Really," said Callie. "I don't want you to be late for work—either of you. If my parents decide to get a pizza for dinner again, I'm going to want it to arrive on time!"

Stevie laughed, but not because she thought anything was very funny. She wasn't about to forget the last time she'd delivered a pizza to Callie's family. In fact, she wished it hadn't happened, but it had. Now she had to find a way to face up to it.

As she pulled out of the airport parking lot, a plane roared overhead, rising into the brooding sky. *Maybe that's Lisa's plane*, she thought. The noise of its flight seemed to mark the beginning of a long summer.

The first splats of rain hit the windshield as Stevie paid their way out of the parking lot. By the time they were on the highway, it was raining hard. The sky had darkened to a steely gray. Streaks of lightning brightened it, only to be followed by thunder that made the girls jump.

The storm had come out of nowhere. Stevie flicked on the windshield wipers and hoped it would go right back to nowhere.

The sky turned almost black as the storm strengthened. Curtains of rain ripped across the windshield, pounding on the hood and roof of the car. The wipers flicked uselessly at the torrent.

"I hope Fez is okay," said Callie. "He hates thunder, you know."

"I'm not surprised," said Carole, trying to control her voice. It seemed to her that there were a lot of things Fez hated. He was as temperamental as any horse she had ever ridden.

Fez was one of the horses in the paddock. Carole didn't want to upset Callie by telling her that. If she told Callie he'd been turned out, Callie would wonder why he hadn't just been exercised. If she told Callie she'd exercised him, Callie might wonder if he was being overworked. Carole shook her head. What was it about this girl that made Carole so certain that whatever she said, it would be wrong? Why couldn't she say the one thing she really needed to say?

Still, Carole worked at Pine Hollow, and that meant taking care of the horses that were boarding there—and that meant keeping the owners happy.

"I'm sure Fez will be fine. Ben and Max will look after him," Carole said.

"I guess you're right," said Callie. "I know he can be difficult. Of course, you've ridden him, so you know that, too. I mean, that's obvious. But it's spirit, you see. Spirit is the key to an endurance specialist. He's got it, and I think he's got the makings of a champion. We'll work together this summer, and come fall . . . well, you'll see."

Spirit—yes, it was important in a horse. Carole knew that. She just wished she understood why it was that Fez's spirit was so irritating to her. She'd always thought of herself as someone who'd never met a horse she didn't like. Maybe it was the horse's owner . . .

"Uh-oh," said Stevie, putting her foot gently on the brake. "I think I got it going a little too fast there."

"You've got to watch out for that," Callie said. "My father says the police practically lie in wait for teenage drivers. They love to give us tickets. Well, they certainly had fun with me."

"You got a ticket?" Stevie asked.

"No, I just got a warning, but it was almost worse than a ticket. I was going four miles over the speed limit in our hometown. The policeman stopped me, and when he saw who I was, he just gave me a warning. Dad was furious—at me and at the officer, though he didn't say anything to the officer. He was angry at him because he thought someone would find out and say I'd gotten special treatment! I was only going four miles over the speed limit. Really. Even the officer said that. Well, it would have been easier if I'd gotten a ticket. Instead, I got grounded. Dad won't let me drive for three months. Of course, that's nothing compared to what happened to Scott last year."

"What happened to Scott?" Carole asked, suddenly curious about the driving challenges of the Forester children.

"Well, it's kind of a long story," said Callie. "But—"

"Wow! Look at that!" Stevie interrupted. There was an amazing streak of lightning over the road ahead. The dark afternoon brightened for a minute. Thunder followed instantly.

"Maybe we should pull off the road or something?" Carole suggested.

"I don't think so," said Stevie. She squinted through the windshield. "It's not going to last long. It never does when it rains this hard. We get off at the next exit anyway."

She slowed down some more and turned the wipers up a notch. She followed the car in front of her, keeping a constant eye on the two red spots of the car's taillights. She'd be okay as long as she could see them. The rain pelted the car so loudly that it was hard to talk. Stevie drove on cautiously.

Then, as suddenly as it had started, the rain stopped. Stevie spotted the sign for their exit, signaled, and pulled off to the right and up the ramp. She took a left onto the overpass and followed the road toward Willow Creek.

The sky was as dark as it had been, and there were clues that there had been some rain there, but nothing nearly as hard as the rain they'd left on the interstate. Stevie sighed with relief and switched the windshield wipers to a slower rate.

"I think I'll drop you off at Pine Hollow first," she said, turning onto the road that bordered the stable's property.

Pine Hollow's white fences followed the contour of the road, breaking the open, grassy hillside into a sequence of paddocks and fields. A few horses stood in the fields, swishing their tails. One bucked playfully and ran up a hill, shaking his head to free his mane in the wind. Stevie smiled. Horses always seemed to her the most welcoming sight in the world.

"Then I'll take Callie home," Stevie continued, "and after that I'll go over to Pizza Manor. I may be a few minutes late for work, but who orders pizza at five o'clock in the afternoon anyway?"

"Now, now," teased Carole. "Is that any way for you to mind your Pizza Manors?"

"Well, at least I have my hat with me," said Stevie. Or did she? She looked into the rearview mirror to see if she could spot it, and when that didn't do any good, she glanced over her shoulder. Callie picked it up and started to hand it to her.

"Here," she said. "We wouldn't want— Wow! I guess the storm isn't over yet!"

The sky had suddenly filled with a brilliant streak of lightning, jagged and pulsating, accompanied by an explosion of thunder.

It startled Stevie. She shrieked and turned her face back to the road. The light was so sudden and so bright that it blinded her for a second. The car swerved. Stevie braked. She clutched at the steering wheel and then realized she couldn't see because the rain was pelting even harder than before. She reached for the wiper control, switching it to its fastest speed.

There was something to her right! She saw something move, but she didn't know what it was.

"Stevie!" Carole cried.

"Look out!" Callie screamed from the backseat.

Stevie swerved to the left on the narrow road, hoping it would be enough. Her answer was a sickening jolt as the car slammed into something solid. The car spun around, smashing against the thing again. When the thing screamed, Stevie knew it was a horse. Then it disappeared from her field of vision. Once again, the car spun. It smashed against the guardrail on the left side of the road and tumbled up and over it as if the rail had never been there.

Down they went, rolling, spinning. Stevie could hear the screams of her friends. She could hear her own voice, echoing in the close confines of the car, answered by the thumps of the car rolling down the hillside into a gully. Suddenly the thumping stopped. The screams were stilled. The engine cut off. The wheels stopped spinning. And all Stevie could hear was the idle *slap*, *slap*, *slap* of her windshield wipers.

"Carole?" she whispered. "Are you okay?"

"I think so. What about you?" Carole answered.

"Me too. Callie? Are you okay?" Stevie asked.

There was no answer.

"Callie?" Carole echoed.

The only response was the girl's shallow breathing.

How could this have happened?

ABOUT THE AUTHOR

Bonnie Bryant is the author of nearly a hundred books about horses, including The Saddle Club series, Saddle Club Super Editions, and the Pony Tails series. She has also written novels and movie novelizations under her married name, B. B. Hiller.

Ms. Bryant began writing The Saddle Club in 1986. Although she had done some riding before that, she intensified her studies then and found herself learning right along with her characters Stevie, Carole, and Lisa. She claims that they are all much better riders than she is.

Ms. Bryant was born and raised in New York City. She still lives there, in Greenwich Village, with her two sons.

Don't miss the next exciting
Saddle Club adventure . . .

SCHOOLING HORSE
Saddle Club #84

A new horse has arrived at Pine Hollow, and Lisa Atwood is convinced that her parents are planning to buy it for her. Of course she volunteers to help school it. But training this horse is a lot more difficult than Lisa thought. In fact, it could be dangerous. How can Lisa tell her parents that she doesn't want *this* horse? And will that mean she'll *never* get a horse of her own?

Meanwhile, Carole Hanson is having schooling problems herself. She's about to fail a course, and she doesn't know where to go for help. Should she try to struggle through? Or just give up?

Can The Saddle Club turn these two schooling disasters into happy endings?